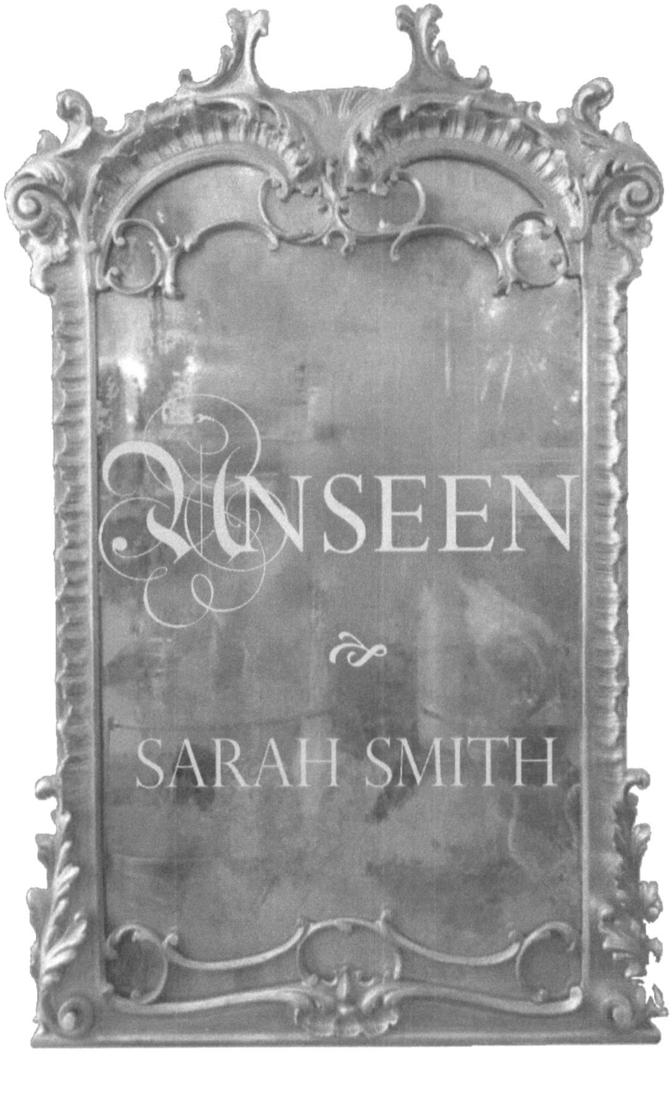

UNSEEN

SARAH SMITH

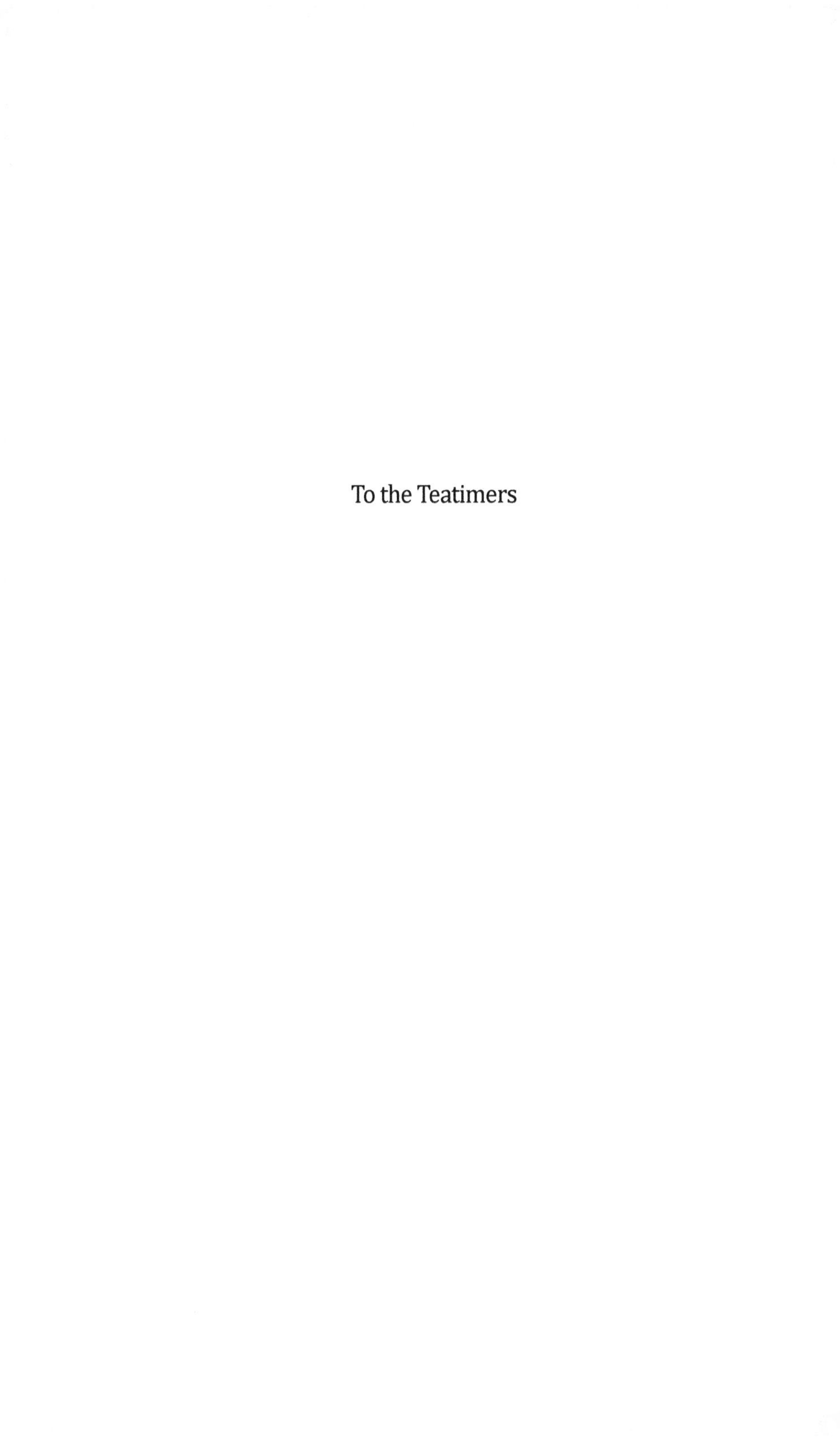

To the Teatimers

Dr. Jules Jouvet, the last Dr. Jouvet, died in his afternoon sleep at the age of ninety-four, on Friday, the third of August, 1906, at the beginning of the long French summer vacation. The rest of the Jouvet staff were already on their way to the country or the beach, to roll their pants legs up or kirtle up their skirts and savor the warmth. His valet had packed Dr. Jouvet's trunk and left too. All Dr. Jouvet would have had to do was phone the taxi. But he lay down for a minute and he died.

Dr. Jouvet would have been going to visit his niece, a middle-aged lady who tolerated this annual disturbance of her cats for the sake of the legacy he'd leave. When he didn't show up on Saturday, the niece worried about him. On Sunday she discussed his absence with the priest, and on Monday with her friends. On Tuesday she went to the pharmacist's and invested in a telephone call to Jouvet Medical Analyses in Paris. No one answered. It took her until Wednesday to nerve herself to take the train the forty miles to Paris; to take the elevator to his top-floor apartment; to enter; to scream; and to have hysterics in the drugstore across the street while the police came.

The niece had liked her uncle well enough and had known what pride he took in his company; but who would take it over?

And so Jouvet Medical Analyses closed, which had been the last hope of the mad and desperate for two hundred years.

ȣ

Alexander Reisden arrived in Paris at the Gare d'Orsay the last week of September, went from the railroad station to the hotel adjoining, and collapsed under the covers. He woke to find his cousin Dotty sitting nervously on his bed, holding the mirror of her compact above his mouth.

"Really, Dotty?" He breathed on the mirror ostentatiously.

She snatched it away. She'd been crying. "You said you'd arrive on Monday and come to dinner Tuesday, and you didn't come and you didn't send a message and I tried to 'phone you and you didn't answer—" She dabbed at her eyes angrily.

"Is it Wednesday?"

"Darling, it *is*. I made them let me in."

"I'm so sorry, darling. Avert your eyes; I'm getting up."

He couldn't give way to guilt and exhaustion: not for Dotty's sake, not for his. He needed to be robustly healthy, physically and mentally, for the sake of the new job, for Paris.

In the bathroom, he dry-swallowed aspirin, stretched his stiff arm, and grimaced. "I'm taking a bath," he called through the door. "Find me clothes?"

"Darling, your luggage is full of *papers.*"

"Lab notes." He eased himself into the hot bath. The scar on his shoulder burned and his ribs ached.

"Dearest. Is *everything* you own black?"

Dead black, darling. Mourning black. Suitable for what he'd found out about himself. "It doesn't matter what I wear."

"Oh, honestly, darling. Have you forgot you're in Paris?" She half-opened the door to leave a neatly folded pile of clothes on the bathroom chair. The folds somehow indicated disapproval. She closed the door again without looking at him. When had she got to be body-shy with him? She didn't want to see the scars, he supposed.

He didn't want to show them.

He shaved and dressed and came out, smiling at her. "Come to breakfast with me? I'm starved."

"Darling, it's past eleven."

"Lunch, then."

"Come to dinner tonight. You can meet my Tiggy."

Tiggy was her son, three years old. "Yes, I'd like that."

"And," she added nervously, "I shall have a favor to ask you."

Oh? Dotty's favors were seldom easy.

〝

He called the Physiological Psychology Lab. "This is Dr. Alexander Reisden. I'm your new man at the lab. There should be five boxes of lab equipment for me."

They hadn't arrived yet.

"When they do, would you get them to my bench and send me a message at the Hôtel d'Orsay?"

He should have brought all of his microscope with him. He'd brought its optics, but shipped the body of the scope. It was custom-built: Bausch and Lomb Grand Continental body, Zeiss mechanical stage. He'd picked out the Zeiss lenses himself in London. It meant a great deal to him and it was by far the most expensive thing he owned.

Nothing would happen to it, he told himself.

He wouldn't be able to do lab work without it. He wouldn't be able to see.

❧

Dotty's boy should have a gift. What does one get for a three-year-old child? What did children want?

He asked the hotel concierge for advice and was sent to Au Paradis des enfants, the big toy store on the rue de Rivoli. Even on a Wednesday afternoon, mothers and children were shopping. Toys were piled up everywhere, hundreds of them. He had no memory of owning a toy and no idea what they were for. Wooden blocks to make a fort. Did small boys want to make a fort? Toy horns and drums; too noisy? Dotty's husband had nerves.

He stood, shoulders hunched, hands in pockets, in the midst of all this familial shopping. This was the sort of errand he'd send someone else on.

In America last summer, he would have asked Perdita.

Not an option now.

A sigh on the wall advertised *Steiff animals this way.* Even he had heard of Steiff animals. Stuffed bears, donkeys on wheels, no sharp edges; suitable? He rounded the corner—

A child screamed. A woman called out "Murderer!"

His shoulders squared defensively; then *no,* he told himself, *don't be dramatic, it's not about you,* and he turned to look behind him.

The woman behind him was dressed in deepest mourning. They matched: his black, hers. She was approaching the exhibit of Steiff toys like Death entering a children's party. Children hid in their mothers' skirts, staring at her.

A mother hissed at her. "How dare you come here!"

A shop assistant bustled up. "Good afternoon, Madame la duchesse! I'll be glad to assist you." Doing his best to make her welcome, or more likely get rid of her. "Another order for the orphans?"

"Yes." The woman's voice was hoarse and low, as if she seldom spoke; but she sounded young. She wore unrelieved black, the extravagant black a chief mourner would have worn at a Victorian funeral. Her veil was thick and fell past her shoulders. The black was slightly faded. She had been in hiding behind that veil for a long time.

The shop assistant took out an order pad. "For the orphans," he repeated, as if he could somehow write the children's fear and the mothers' accusations away.

"Twenty-one Steiff bears," the young woman in black said. "Sixteen sets of building blocks, thirty-six spinning tops, fifteen dolls."

"Ah, yes," one of the mothers whispered, "spend your money! It won't help you when the police come for you!"

"Shall we send them directly to the orphanage, madame?"

"No, to my father's. I will send everything in one of my father's trucks."

She was wearing black gloves and didn't take them off to sign the bill. Behind her veil, what he could see of her face was white and unnaturally set, like a mask.

The assistant showed her out, unobtrusively placing himself between her and the mothers.

The assistant helped him decide between a donkey and a Teddy bear. He almost asked about the woman in black, but he felt their eyes on him, the women with their children. What was a man alone doing here, a man who knew nothing about toys, buying a toy for a child he had never met?

He almost flinched, the way the woman in black had.

Murderer.

❧

If you're going to confess to murder, don't muddy it by confessing to the wrong one first.

The murder he'd thought he'd committed had been an accident.

He knew that now.

But last summer he'd found out—no, Gilbert Knight and Perdita and he together had found out why he thought he'd committed murder.

Simplest explanation in the world, really.

He had.

It had been, on the whole, a justifiable murder. Self-defense, even though he'd probably wanted to do it—He'd been eight years old. He didn't remember whether he'd wanted to do it.

It had been less justifiable to run away afterward.

Now what?

He couldn't go back. To explain at all, he'd have had to confess to the murder.

He'd had the summer with Gilbert and Perdita: his only living real relative, the girl he'd unexpectedly fallen in love with. He wouldn't drag them through the newspapers. And he probably wouldn't have been believed. After all, he had already confessed to one murder he hadn't done, and that had got him declared insane; it would simply have looked as though he were getting in the habit.

No, he was doomed to stay himself. Dotty's adopted cousin, Alexander von Reisden. Who had been in an asylum, as everyone remembered.

Who now had the job of convincing Paris and the very prestigious Laboratoire de psychologie physiologique that he was sane, normal, ordinary.

He had no idea how he could.

Ȕ

"Do something for me," Dotty told him.

That night he went to Dotty's. He met Tiggy, a stocky little blond charmer who gravely accepted his Teddy bear. ("What will you name him, darling?" Dotty asked. "Bear," said Tiggy, clutching it round the neck and looking up at him distrustfully. Hello, Tiggy, here's your insane uncle.)

They left Tiggy in the nursery and had dinner in Dotty's large, perfect dining room, only the two of them. Esmé was nowhere to be seen. After dinner she sat him down in the drawing room by the fire, he in her husband's leather club chair, and she perched on a gilded bergère chair.

"Did Tiggy like the bear?" Reisden asked. He had no idea.

"Oh, I'm sure, darling."

No help. "Give me guidance next time. I'm lost with children."

There was something missing, he realized, apart from Esmé. Esmé was a hunter; there were always a couple of dogs underfoot. "Shall we see Esmé?"

"Esmé will be gone for a while," she said stiffly. "He's exploring. In Egypt." Esmé? Egypt? Exploring? Esmé, Monte Carlo, baccarat, more likely. She changed the subject briskly. "What's happened to your arm?" It ached too much to conceal entirely.

"Tattoo gone wrong.—What's happened to the dogs? Did Esmé take them with him?"

"Oh, those dogs," she said, not answering.

No dogs. No smell of dogs. Esmé had been gone for some time.

"What was the favor you wanted?" he asked.

"Darling," she said, "find me a way to make money."

"Doesn't Esmé give you enough?"

"I want some independence."

Had Esmé gone bankrupt? Left her for a can-can dancer?

"I can't just give you money?" he suggested.

"I really want to make my own." She leaned forward. "Darling, are you well? Because if you are, I want to do a project with you."

He raised internal eyebrows. "I'm fine, but I'm working."

"This will amuse you.—Darling, do you still play the stock market? How rich are you now?"

"Rolling in it, I suppose. I don't have my own lab to fund and I don't have any instrumentation to buy until Zeiss invents the next thing. Nothing to spend on but Teddy bears. I should find an investment."

"Would you like to buy a building?"

Well, that was unexpected. "Darling, do I do real estate?"

"Don't you remember, years and years ago, I found that sweet little house by the sea? You put up the money, I did all the work, and we made scads of money from it?"

"We were sixteen, Dots! We didn't know what we were doing."

"But everyone was so impressed with us."

"You bought jewelry with your profits," he remembered.

She touched her pearls. "You used yours to escape," she said. "And Tiggy and I want—Well, darling, I do want money."

Whatever it was with Esmé, Dotty wouldn't talk until she was ready; he knew her.

"I have a building in mind," she continued. "A perfect location, just off the St.-Germain. It'll need everything; it's been a doctor's office and a laboratory. But it's large. One could make six flats out of it. It's not far from your hotel. You could go there, see if it looks right."

"I do have a job," he said. "But I'll take a look and if you do the work, I'll front you."

She hesitated. "I should say— It was Jouvet Medical Analyses."

"And?"

"They treated mad people, darling."

For a moment he felt angry and sad, and suppressed it. She was right to warn him. "And?"

She looked at him for a moment almost guiltily. "You're sure? You really don't mind?"

"I'm sure whatever building troubles there are, I'll foist on you."

"It will give Paris something to talk about," Dotty speculated. "When they talk about you —"

"Rather than what they would say?" he agreed.

"Darling?" She hesitated. "It will be…reassuring. To turn the building to other uses."

"Tell me that's not why we're doing it."

"We're doing it to make me independent," she said.

❧

His crates arrived at the lab the next morning. Just in time; this was Thursday and he was scheduled to do his introductory presentation on Friday.

Like all labs, Physio.Psych. had no privacy and precious little space. Researchers worked elbow to elbow. His bench was toward the middle of the room, with the packing cases with his equipment piled on it. As he made his way to it, there was a little echoing silence.

"You're the one who had the breakthrough about muscle motion!" his neighbor said, too heartily.

"Let's hope I did; now I have to prove it. I'm Alexander Reisden. Hello."

He smiled, but his attention wasn't on it; he'd seen what was waiting for him on his lab bench.

He'd sent five cases.

Only four had arrived.

And he knew instantly which one was missing.

"Did a fifth case arrive? Does the porter have it?" he said, trying to sound calm.

He spent the rest of the morning first with the porter confirming that the case hadn't arrived, then at the railroad Lost Property Office, going through the freight and filling out forms.

Missing, one wooden freight case, about two feet by three, covered in "Fragile" stickers.

Contents, a microscope.

Yes, insured.

Yes, for that much.

No, not replaceable.

He had three years of data with this microscope; he knew perfectly how far to believe it. Not replaceable at all.

He sent a telegram to his ex-lab assistant in Switzerland—*did my microscope end up back there? Would you trace it from your end?*—and then, because he'd been helping move boxes, his arm announced it'd be good for nothing for the rest of the day. He went back to the hotel, took a pain pill, and stared at the ceiling.

For distraction, he reworked his presentation for tomorrow. *I'm Reisden, I study the biochemistry of voluntary muscle motion. This is my hand; how does it move?* His work combined pure chemical experiments and microscope work, at the limits of the resolution of visible light. He could talk about his theories, about working with dark-field lighting to visualize them.

He'd hoped to demonstrate his setup, with the microscope at the middle of it.

He'd *shipped* the d—n thing, not kept it with him.

Yes, he'd been shot, but did he not care about his instrument?

He dragged himself into the bathroom to practice in front of a mirror. Looked at himself in the mirror. Tried a smile.

He could do this. He had to.

❧

He gave his introductory chalk talk Friday afternoon in front of the other lab men; it went well enough, all standard for a new man in a big lab. Except that he had no setup to demonstrate, and he felt he was radiating panic about his lost scope.

He wasn't the only one presenting. A very young graduate student named Michel Fourche had run into a major difficulty in his research work. Fourche did longitudinal studies of madness that ran in families. (Whenever the word *madness* was spoken, everyone carefully did not look at Reisden.) Fourche had been working with a large medical archive associated with a lab. The lab had abruptly closed and the archives were no longer available. Fourche had clearly never faced anything more daunting.

Reisden asked a neutral question or two. How did Fourche know that the same madness showed up in successive generations? Data from a hundred years ago must be unreliable.

"Jouvet used to describe symptoms. They might have called it wandering wits, but—"

Jouvet?

They treated mad people, Dotty had said. Jouvet had been the owner of the building Dotty was trying to buy.

After the end of the session, he asked Fourche a few carefully casual questions. "We're buying their building."

"You've never heard of Jouvet?" Fourche said. "Sherlock Holmes for medical mysteries. Old Dr. Jouvet was a great diagnostician, brilliant until the day he died. Madness a specialty. And now Jouvet's gone."

Fourche blushed when he said *madness.*

"Sad. He might have helped when I broke down," Reisden said steadily. Best to get that over with.

Fourche blinked. "I— I didn't mean to pry, I'm sorry—"

No, child, I mean you to hear this and pass it on. "I do talk about it. I had a breakdown and tried to kill myself. It was almost six years ago, it hurt like a bastard, it was messy and embarrassing, and I will never, never do it again."

He winced inwardly for everyone's sake, including his own.

"You didn't—?" Fourche said.

"Didn't what?"

"I mean— You don't look well."

"Oh, my arm? Yes, it still hurts. Tragically embarrassing. A cow bit me. Did you even know they do that? Berthet wouldn't have hired me if I were trying to hurt myself."

"You're a genius, he might have," Fourche blurted, and blushed red. "Anyway," he said desperately, "the niece who inherited won't even talk to me about the archives! I don't know what to do!"

"Don't give up," he said. "You might help someone."

"Jouvet might have helped someone," Fourche said bitterly. "Me, I'm only doing the autopsy. And now I have to find something else to do.—You're buying the building?"

"Possibly. My cousin and I."

"Is there any way you could talk to the niece about the archives?"

He walked back via the busy Boulevard St.-Germain toward his hotel. He stopped for a coffee at the Café des Deux Magots and watched the normal happy people strolling past. Since he'd been in Paris last, the women's hats had got huge and half the taxis were electric instead of horse-drawn. There were posters everywhere for plays he didn't know. Exercise would help him; he would heal; he'd find his microscope and do chemistry. Right now he felt—oh, probably no more than nerves at meeting new people; but he felt shaken, as sick of himself as everyone certainly was of him.

The Jouvet building was at the corner of the rue de l'Université, a gray stone hulk, much older than the buildings around it, spilling shadow over the street. Outside, a moving van waited with a patient horse exploring its nose-bag. The courtyard door stood open into an electric-lit yard.

Inside, a war was going on. A man with the muscles of a mover was balancing a file cabinet on the steps, about to heave it out of the building. Two men, one old, one some sort of teenaged apprentice, were hanging off him, trying to stop him. A provincial woman in crackling-new mourning was standing in the courtyard, screaming at them all.

"I'll have them all out!" she was shrieking. "It's my right! I'm selling the building!"

"Give them back! They aren't yours!" Another woman, a clerkly woman with greying hair, stood on the steps flourishing, of all things, a cavalry sword.

"*Mais si*, they are!"

Madame Clerk hefted the sword and pointed it at Madame Mourning. "They belong to Jouvet!"

"I'm burning them!" the countrywoman shouted. "I'm not afraid of you, Mme Herschner!" She ducked forward and tugged one of the file drawers away from the mover. "Look!" she said, pulling out folders tied in red tape and scattering them over the cobblestones.

He was looking at the Jouvet archives.

"They're gone! I'm burning them right here!" She kicked the folders together and took a tin match-holder out of her purse, struck a match, and dropped it into the pile of paper.

He stepped forward, into the courtyard, and crushed the creeping fire under his heel.

"Who are *you*?" the countrywoman said.

"Who are you?" said Madame Clerk.

He pushed the sword away with one finger.

"I'm from the Laboratoire de psychologie physiologique at the École de médicine," he said, "and I'm here to look at the building. But I want the archives too. Do put down that sword."

❧

"Darling. You're going to buy the *company*?"

"We get the building for less if I take the company with it. Otherwise the niece has to clear out the archives. Which take up the entire basement."

"But clearing out, that'll be a horrible job."

"Someone at Physio.Psych. will do it; he wants the archives. For the rest, I'll look at the equipment and see if it's worth getting an auctioneer in. Everything else goes to the junk man. Whom you will arrange for, darling. I wind up the company and you do the renovations."

"Perhaps you could use the equipment?"

"I'll take a look, but no."

"Have you found your microscope yet?"

"No, darling."

They were in the library, after dinner. He was sitting in Esmé's leather chair again. There was a pronounced absence of Esmé.

"It may have been stolen," he admitted. "The railroad police think so."

"Who would steal a microscope?"

"It's worth as much as a race-car. If it's ended up in a mont-de-piété and someone's bought it for their spotty child, I shall be really annoyed."

"As much as an *automobile?*"

"Let's not talk about it."

Darling, let's talk about what's happened with your husband, shall we? Reisden had spent a half hour or so upstairs with Tiggy before dinner, doing his best not to be frightening. Tiggy had smiled at him. Tiggy's nursemaid had asked indignantly whether he was an uncle on Monsieur's side of the family? When he said Madame's, the nursemaid had warmed to him, though only slightly.

Tiggy had said he missed the dogs. "They went with Daddy." Reisden had almost asked how long the dogs had been gone, and restrained himself. One doesn't pry gossip out of children.

"Why does anyone want the archives?" Dotty asked.

"Generational studies of madness."

"Oh, madness, darling—" She looked away from him, at the fireplace.

Oh, bugger, he was sick of being mad.

"Don't rob me of my good deed," he said.

∽

Was it a good deed? Giving away the archives was easy. He consulted with Berthet: Once Jouvet was his and the company was dissolved, he would donate the archives to Physio.Psych.

Telling Fourche didn't go as well.

"You'll need to find storage for them," Reisden said.

"But—"

"No, that will be your job. Part of your training. When you have a lab, you'll always need to raise money."

Fourche swallowed. "Who gives money for storage?"

"That's the first part of your training."

They visited the Jouvet archives. In the musty basement, darkness and squeaks scuttled away from their flashlights. Fourche stared in terror at the rows of filing cabinets stretching away into the dark. From on top of one cabinet, a well-fed cat narrowed green eyes at them.

"Oh L—d," Fourche said.

At the top of the stairs, Dr. Jouvet's old secretary, the woman who had held the niece off with a sword, was waiting for them.

"It would be easier to keep Jouvet open," Mme Herschner said. She held out a folder for him. "And we could do it, Monsieur de Reisden, I have the figures here. You would actually earn more if we continued as a medical building—I would be glad to show you."

"But who would be Dr. Jouvet?" Fourche said.

"Fourche couldn't organize his own socks," he said to Dotty, "and the Jouvet employees want to keep Jouvet going."

"You won't let them, will you?"

"No."

He and Dotty were sitting at Dotty's mahogany dining-room table on Sunday afternoon, going over figures. The building inspector had been by; the building was ancient, shabby, and outdated, but it wouldn't fall tomorrow. Dr. Jouvet's niece had accepted his first offer. All she'd wanted was her uncle's china and silver and the family photographs.

"It's so good, darling," Dotty said. "You're going to help me make a mint."

"I suppose." He sat back in the chair, tapping his pencil, discontented.

"But?"

He looked for some way to tell her *You're distracting me from what I should be doing.* Not only the building. He'd checked up; Esmé was gone. Not in Paris and not at his country house. Reisden had gone as far as to read the society pages in the Sorbonne library. Esmé hadn't appeared in the lists of participants in his usual stag hunts or fox hunts. Esmé wouldn't miss the hunting season.

And Dotty wasn't talking.

On the floor, under the table, little Tiggy was playing. Reisden had a sense that children were supposed to enjoy themselves. Tiggy was quiet and sad; Dotty chattered, gossipy and breakable.

Esmé had left her and she was lying about it; what was she lying about?

He offered up his own frustrations as an invitation to her.

"Physio.Psych.," he said. "I think Berthet oversold me. Half of them seem to think I'm the new resident genius, which appalls me."

"But, darling, you are a genius."

"Ffft. I had a good idea. But I'm working with a crippled lab setup. I've borrowed one of the lab microscopes and it might as well be binoculars." She looked baffled. "I'm a carpenter without a hammer. I want *my* machine. The police can't find it. If it's really gone, should I give up dealing with Bausch & Lomb because I can get a Zeiss body faster? Or there's the Zeiss UV—" She was looking at him as if he were saying *mimble mimble*. "Sorry," he said.

All the mechanics of losing it made him heartsick: decisions, waiting, looking *stupid* for losing it.

"And it'll take Fourche bloody forever to find storage for the archives. He hasn't a clue and I won't get involved.

Meanwhile—" He got up and looked out Dotty's dining room window. Downstairs, past the men fishing on the quai, the brown Seine ran untroubled; it knew where it was going. "Where's Physio.Psych. in this, where's chemistry, when do I stop faffing about and *settle*? Dotty, I feel—"

Not normal yet? Say anything of the sort and people would start watching him carefully. "I feel frustrated. Not settled." He thumped his palm against the windowsill once, took a deep breath, and came back to the table. "And that's my tantrum for today."

"Darling, what can I do?"

"Find me somewhere to live, won't you? It's pathetic I'm still in a railway hotel. I need an apartment. Somewhere in the Fifth. Small, walkable to Physio.Psych."

"Darling, no one lives in the Fifth, only students. It'll have to be the Sixth."

"Small, walkable," he conceded.

"You know," she said, "there's an apartment in *our* building, on the top floor. Dr. Jouvet's old apartment. Have you seen it?"

He shook his head. All he knew was it existed and Dr. Jouvet had died there. Not a recommendation.

But practical, and he'd move once Dotty brought the builders in.

"If it's not a pit, it'll do for now."

"Though really, darling—" Dotty shook her head. "Jouvet. Madmen. Perhaps you shouldn't live there?"

"It'll be fine, Dotty, I only need someplace to spread my papers."

❧

On Friday afternoon he signed the documents that put him in official possession of the building, the archives, and the company; and that night he moved in.

He'd hoped the building would be deserted. It wasn't. All the soon-to-be-former staff had showed up. In the analytics lab, the techs were lined up at their benches, earnest men with untrimmed beards, women in sensible blouses and skirts. In the staff room, Mme Herschner introduced him to "the experts," Jouvet's consultants, who looked as though they'd been gathered randomly from the street. One was dressed to go to the opera and said he sorted data. One, smoking a cigar and scattering ashes, was some sort of psychoanalyst. One did autopsies. Those he could understand. But the tramp? The chestnut seller? The accordion player?

The elderly woman in the red dress, veiled as thickly as Madame Death at the Paradis des enfants?

"We all would like to know," said Mme Herschner, "what your plans are for Jouvet."

"There are no plans for Jouvet. I've bought the company to close it up."

"But the figures I gave you—"

"Are irrelevant, I'm afraid."

"I would be glad to discuss that, Monsieur de Reisden."

You're all fired. Those are my plans.

Give them the weekend.

Give himself the weekend.

"You'll all hear more on Monday. Go home."

Most of them did. Some of the techs kept working—"we still have cases, Monsieur" —while Mme Herschner showed him round.

The waiting room, the nurses' station, the interview rooms with the diplomas on the walls, the smells of disinfectant and anxiety: those brought back memories he'd rather lose. When he'd been persuading people he could still be trusted around chemicals, he'd spent hours in rooms like this. He'd stared at other walls, other diplomas, being asked questions he couldn't answer.

Up in the lab area, he felt easier; the setup reminded him of Physio.Psych. The Jouvet lab wasn't bad at all: well-organized test benches, up-to-date equipment, even a neurological test lab with instruments Physio.Psych. wouldn't scorn. The scopes weren't up to his but were more than adequate.

Jouvet didn't look as if it had been run by a near-centenarian.

Mme Herschner showed him Dr. Jouvet's office, which was dignified and old-fashioned. ("It reassures our clients.") Shelves of thirty-year-old medical tomes crowded the glassed-in bookcases, together with a few medical exhibits and what Mme Herschner said was a famous skull. The usual clients' chairs faced Dr. Jouvet's imposing desk, but to one side of the room, by the fireplace, sat two chairs. "If the case called for great sympathy, Monsieur, Dr. Jouvet and the client would sit there."

Along one wall, where Dr. Jouvet had been able to see them from his desk, hung five portraits. Five Dr. Jouvets: five great diagnosticians, from the French Revolutionary doctor to the man just dead. The last Dr. Jouvet had been painted in middle age: a kind face, welcoming eyes behind heavy glasses, head tilted a bit to one side, as if he were just about to say *Tell me all about it. Tell me everything.*

For a moment Reisden wished he could tell Dr. Jouvet everything, could talk out his awkward life with someone else. He wished he had something encouraging to say to the hopeful techs who wanted to keep Jouvet going. But Dr. Jouvet, their great diagnostician, was dead, and without him Jouvet Medical Analyses was just another lab.

"Would you like to see the apartment now, Monsieur?"

One of the bookcases in Dr. Jouvet's office was a secret door. Behind it, a staircase led up to Dr. Jouvet's apartment. Even from the staircase, it was clear the apartment would be less reassuring than the lab. As Mme Herschner climbed the stairs in front of him, her long skirt brushed the wall and flakes of whitewash dropped off.

Downstairs, Jouvet had electric light. Up here was gaslight. She lit a match and turned on the gas. It flickered and hissed, revealing chaos. Perhaps a hundred unopened packages of books crowded the small foyer: some of them unopened for so long their postage stamps had faded.

"He let himself go a bit up here, Monsieur." Mme Herschner looked a bit dismayed. "He did like books."

Good G-d, he did. Reisden had brought a flashlight. He opened a door: sitting room. Books were piled haphazardly against every wall. Rows of green Egyptian grave-figurines lined the windowsills. Curiosities crowded the mantelpiece, the tables, the floor; the walls were three deep in pictures, dark daubs in the flashlight beam.

"He would take payment in art from artists," Mme Herschner said. She trailed off and sneezed. "It's dusty, I'm afraid. We haven't really done anything... Let me show you the rest of the apartment."

She moved through the rest of it, lighting the gas, which popped and hissed and glared yellow. The tiny kitchen might produce a cup of coffee. The WC and bath were...there. He tested the WC by pulling the chain and the tank didn't fall off the wall, which counted as a pass.

"Let me show you Dr. Jouvet's bedroom. You may want it; it's the best. It has a view of the Eiffel Tower."

By now he'd heard how the man had died. He stopped her from even lighting the gas and shone his flashlight inside, briefly. The bed was stripped down to the frame. The rest was occupied by Dr. Jouvet's absence. A bathrobe folded on a chair. More books and a pair of dusty glasses on the bedside table. Dr. Jouvet's trunk was open against the wall, packed for a summer trip. After three months, any smell was almost certainly his imagination, but—

"Decidedly not."

❧

There were other bedrooms, dauntingly crowded with more of Dr. Jouvet's collections. The apartment was huge and trailed off into darkness. He had Mme Herschner find bedding and towels and then sent her off. He'd had enough of people for today.

He went back into the sitting room and turned up all the gaslights. He'd need a desk. Dr. Jouvet had a good-sized work desk up here; it was piled with unread magazines and notes from grateful patients. He found a bin and began sweeping everything from the desk into it: the notes of thanks, *you have saved me,* all the bits and pieces of a life that had meant something, going to the trash. *Dr. Jouvet is dead. The company is closing.* He went into the kitchen to make himself coffee, but of course he hadn't brought coffee so there wasn't any. He drank a cup of water standing by the sink, came back, and emptied the desk drawers into the bin without looking at any of their contents.

One thing done.

He had to do something about the books, but by now his arm was telling him to take a rest. He found a decent chair and dragged it over to the gas fireplace. Setting it where he wanted it, he looked up and was genuinely spooked: facing him across the fireplace was what had to be Dr. Jouvet's reading chair, with piles of half-read books around it.

If the case called for great sympathy, Dr. Jouvet would sit with the client.

He found a box in the kitchen and piled the litter of Dr. Jouvet's books into it, and looked for someplace to put them out of sight, hoping the ghost of Dr. Jouvet would disappear with them. Across the room, covering what looked like an alcove, hung a pair of faded velvet curtains. He pulled one back and used his flashlight to see what he'd found.

It was the entrance to another room, a music room. And in the center of it was a piano.

And there was a ghost sitting at the piano bench: not Dr. Jouvet's, but his own.

He could see Perdita playing the piano. He could *hear* her: the Schumann she'd been working on last summer, soft and bright and dazzling. Perdita, the way she held her hands over the piano, as if she was about to discover something entirely new; the music, the very sound of her breath; she was more real than anything in his life since last summer; *oh Perdita—* He touched the piano, hoping to feel the vibrations of music, and found himself kneeling on the floor, his head in his hands.

Which was alarming. Very. He couldn't miss her that much; he couldn't afford to. He gave himself a moment, then stood up and dusted himself off. Somewhere in Paris, some time, it was inevitable he'd run across a piano and be reminded of her. At least he hadn't done it in public. He pulled the curtains closed and set a chair in front of them.

It was late. He took himself off to dinner at the loudest, brightest restaurant he could find, brought his evening's work, and wrote it up there. He stayed out late, and would have given quite a bit not to come back to that apartment; but that was nonsense; he was there; he'd stay.

❧

He found three files waiting for him on Dr. Jouvet's desk, marked for *Monsieur le docteur.* Mme Herschner had written, *I would like to consult with you about this difficult case. Dr. Jouvet took on the mystery of Rose Rossi before he died—*

He left them where they were.

Or tried to. He held out through the evening; held out while he was trying to sleep with an aching shoulder in an unfamiliar bed; held out until three in the morning, and then got them, merely for something to read.

Godefroy de St.-Martin, a thick file. *Mathilde de St.-Martin. Rose Rossi,* the thickest of all, full of newspaper clippings. He opened that one first.

Two photographs lay on top. A young woman, a beautiful smiling blonde, presumably Rose Rossi.

And a picture taken from a distance—

He jerked awake.

He knew her. Madame Death in the Paradis des enfants, buying toys for orphans.

Headlines blared at him.

ROSE ROSSI, DID YOU KILL YOUR SON?

❧

"We are delighted that you've invested in us," Mme Herschner said earnestly. It was well before the time when she should have been at the office, but when he came down Dr. Jouvet's secret staircase early the next morning, she was waiting with croissants and coffee.

He wasn't going to let her treat him like her boss.

"I have not invested in Jouvet. The archives will go to Physio.Psych. and the building will be turned into flats. I'm sorry, but that has always been the plan."

"But—" Mme Herschner laid her hand on Madame Death's file. "You read about Rose Rossi, didn't you?"

No. He hadn't even read the rest of the folder.

"She needs the kind of help we can give."

This was clearly intended to have him say *Tell me more.*

Mme Herschner leaned forward. "She's innocent! She called on Dr. Jouvet. Let us help her!"

"I'm sorry."

"Give us two weeks!" Mme Herschner said. "Her mother-in-law is a monster, Monsieur. That woman cares only for the money. It is not only helping her; it is preventing a crime against her."

"Dr. Jouvet can't help her."

"He didn't do everything. Please."

"I'm sorry. The plans are already made."

"But—"

But she would try. He remembered her facing down Dr. Jouvet's niece with a cavalry sword.

"The company will close at the end of the month; that is the plan. But I doubt I could stop you doing whatever you can do, Mme Herschner. A bargain? Don't get in my way and I won't get in yours. You can have your two weeks to solve Dr. Jouvet's last case."

"I would not get in your way," Mme Herschner said, "I work for you now, Monsieur; and when you see what Jouvet can do, you will want all of us to keep working for you."

"No," he said. "I really won't."

❧

"Oh, darling," Dotty said, "I hope you're not tempted to become a rescuer of damsels."

Two chairs on either side of Dotty's fire; they reminded him of Dr. Jouvet's sympathy chairs. They need not; any fire in November had a couple of chairs round it. "Absolutely not," he said.

"Who is she?"

Who, he thought, is Mme Herschner? She had run off to begin her task as lighthearted as a girl, convinced she was going to save the company she had worked for since—he'd asked—since she was twenty-one and newly widowed. Thirty-five years.

"Who is she?" Dotty asked again.

"Oh, sorry; who?"

"This woman who's supposed to be innocent. Who is she?"

"A woman named Rose Rossi."

Dotty gasped. "*Rose Rossi?* Darling, Jouvet is trying to solve the case of *Rose Rossi?*"

"Jouvet is not. Do you know her?"

"Only the most notorious murderer or the most innocent victim in Paris! It's such a mystery!"

"I really don't want to hear," he said.

"Darling, you do, you do, you do."

Several years ago, the multimillionaire grocer Charles.Rossi had decided that his beautiful only child, Rose, should marry a title. He'd made known to Parisian society that his daughter's dowry would be enough to catch a duke, and he'd actually got one: the penniless Godefroy de St.-Martin.

Godefroy de St.-Martin had first come to the attention of Jouvet at six, when he had attempted to burn his mother's lapdog alive. The analyst who'd talked with him had warned Mathilde de St.-Martin that her son wouldn't stop there. She'd told the analyst that he was wrong, and got a bigger dog.

Godefroy had a special interest in fire. At thirteen he'd used a fork to brand a kitchen-maid at his school. His mother had taken him out of school and arranged for tutoring.

(It had been the analyst's opinion that, while Godefroy was torturing women with fire, his mother would have held his coat and passed the matches.)

When Godefroy turned twenty-one, his mother had gone looking for a rich young girl who didn't know Parisian gossip. There she was, Rose Rossi, the grocer's daughter, sixteen and innocent as milk. Mathilde de St.-Martin pounced.

After the marriage, Mathilde arranged for Godefroy to take up a remote position as a trader representing French companies in the Moyen-Congo, upriver from Brazzaville. Godefroy and Rose were the only Europeans at the outpost.

("The *Congo*, darling," Dotty said, "you know what *that* means." Their cousin Sigi was an attaché at Léopoldville, and they had all read Conrad. The horror, the horror.)

Rose had given birth to a son, Philippe. But, eighteen months after her son's birth, Rose appeared at Brazzaville, alone.

"Without her husband, darling," Dotty said, "and *without her son*."

According to Rose, Godefroy had begun to torture the village women. She feared for her life and Philippe's. She'd written to her father. She wanted to leave her husband, take her boy, and request *séparation de biens.*

That is, Rose would take with her not only the heir but the money she'd brought to the marriage.

According to Rose, Godefroy had discovered the letter and had set fire to their house, with all of them in it. Rose had escaped the fire; her husband and son had died. But she'd been burned. Even in Brazzaville, which is always hot and humid, she wore a thick veil. She said she would never show her face again.

"She *said* she was burned," Dotty said.

"I've seen her," Reisden said. That black figure. The thick veil. The white, set face underneath, as if she were wearing a mask. "When she signed the bill, she had trouble holding the pen."

"But Godefroy's mother says that she isn't burned at all. She's only pretending."

"Why?"

"For the dowry," Dotty said. "So everyone will be sorry for her and not ask *when* Philippe died."

"You're going to tell me why that's important."

"Darling, it's succession law. Rose's dowry was a share in Rossi's Fine Groceries. A *large* share. In France, the estate of a dead man belongs to the husband's family and the wife gets almost nothing," Dotty made a face. He sat up a bit, watching her. Where was Esmé, and why did Dotty want money of her own? "But Rose's father was a good businessman and wrote the terms of her dowry. If her husband died *and left no heir*, Rose would get her dowry back.

"So who died first?" Dotty asked. "Her husband or her son? If her son died first, the Rossis will be free of the hideous St.-Martins. If not, Mathilde de St.-Martin will almost *own* Rossi's Groceries."

According to Rose, she had been in the main room of their house with Philippe in her arms when Godefroy had snatched Philippe, shaken him, tossed him onto the floor, and thrown a lamp at Rose. Screaming, with her long blonde hair alight and the room already beginning to burn, Rose had dodged him, thrown a chair at him, and managed to pick up Philippe and run outside. The two had been taken to the local hospital, but there, Philippe had been pronounced already dead.

In the meantime, the house had collapsed. Godefroy's body had been recovered from the ruins the next morning.

The child, the child: he thought of the child. He could see that room full of the psychopathic rage of the man, the casual way he'd shaken the child and tossed him aside, and the room burning.

"So," Dotty said with an air of triumph, "did Philippe die after Godefroy?"

French lawyers had been arguing the case in the papers. When two people have died together, the *Code civil* is a morass. Usually the weaker was supposed to have died first; if a child and a father died together, the child was presumed to have died first. And if Rose's testimony was right, Godefroy might actually have killed his son.

In either case, Godefroy would have left no living heirs and Rose would have her dowry back. But when did Philippe die? When his father threw him on the floor? From smoke inhalation? After the house collapsed, at the hospital, when Godefroy was already dead?

The answer was worth millions.

Mathilde de St.-Martin had hired a French private investigator in the Congo. The detective was getting an order to exhume Philippe. "Apparently one can tell if someone dies in a fire?" Dotty said.

"Smoke in the lungs," he said automatically.

She looked at him. "Darling, please don't know those things.—Anyway, when Philippe is dug up, if he died in the fire, Mathilde will get the money. If he died because of Godefroy, Rose will get the money. But Mathilde says he died later. After the fire. Mathilde says Rose smothered him because she didn't want to be burdened with him. Darling, you look pale."

"Child-murder doesn't bother *you?*" he exploded. "Sorry, Dotty. I'm sorry."

"Well, of course it does, but— Rose goes to an esthetician here in Paris. Mathilde says that as soon as Rose is sure of her money, the esthetician is going to effect a miraculous 'cure', and there Rose will be, rich and pretty and unencumbered. *Let her answer questions!* Mathilde will say.

Let the grocer's daughter say what happened to my grandson! In open court!

"Is she burned? I think not! Let Rose remove her veil and show herself!"

The fire popped in the grate. Reisden reached for the brandy bottle and poured himself a double.

"And everyone in Paris is looking forward to her testifying," he said. "Because people are cruel."

"Curious, darling. They're only curious."

He shook his head. "What do you think happened?"

"I do hate to agree with Mathilde, but I think Rose isn't as badly burned as she makes out. She goes to an esthetician, darling; a woman doesn't go to be made beautiful if she's a scaly horror. What do you think?"

He wasn't going to get involved. Not for Rose Rossi's sake; not for Mme Herschner, who thought Rose was innocent, or Dotty, who wanted the building.

But he'd think about it, at night in that haunted apartment—

"Do you keep in touch with Sigi at Léopoldville?" he asked.

"Of course, darling, don't you?"

He kept in touch with no one. "Does he know people in Brazzaville? Telegraph him and ask him to check the story. That much we can do."

❧

He read the file.

One further thing, and not reassuring. Rose Rossi's file included the original letter from Charles Rossi, hiring Jules Jouvet. And reading between the lines, it was clear that the millionaire grocer doubted his daughter's story, and didn't want to.

She behaves as if she's guilty, Rossi had written to Dr. Jouvet. *Which she is not!* he'd added immediately. *I know it!*

Or only hope it?

I cannot believe my daughter could do what people have said about her, Charles Rossi had written Jules Jouvet. *She is innocent! Please, Dr. Jouvet, help her to find peace.*

He remembered Rose Rossi at the Paradis des enfants, shrinking away from the mothers and their children.

She hadn't found peace, whatever she'd done.

Least of all if she were a murderer trying to act innocent; he knew about that.

No one had saved Philippe.

And no one, except Mme Herschner, was going to save her.

❧

Mme Herschner was at her desk, talking on the telephone. A small orchid drooped by her ink-bottle and a chipped vase held a single rose. "Jouvet is closing," she told the caller, in the voice of a woman who was telling a child it could not have a kitten because Reisden had drowned them all. They closed themselves in Dr. Jouvet's office and went over plans for laying off staff. Two techs would be needed to run the last of the analyses; Mme Herschner would do the secretarial work and filing herself; the rest— She took out her handkerchief and dabbed at her eyes, then sat very straight and folded her hands.

She was working on a plan for Rose Rossi, she said. She'd consult with him on it in a day or so.

"You're sure she's innocent, Madame? Her father doesn't seem to think so."

"I am sure she needs to be helped."

"Helped," he said. "Either her husband turned her into a burnt nightmare and killed her son, or she killed her son. Is there anything you can do for her?"

"Bring her back into the world."

"Is that a kindness?" he thought out loud.

"I don't say a kindness, Monsieur. But it's the only thing!"

❧

That day he had his first official meeting with the head of Physio.Psych., his new boss, Berthet.

"How are you doing so far?"

"I'm letting you down," he said.

"Are you?"

"I show up with the best part of my equipment missing, I don't have an adequate setup, and I distract myself by buying a building."

Not to mention brooding about a murder.

They were in Berthet's office: desk on one side, on the other two leather chairs grouped companionably next to a fireplace. Dr. Jouvet's sympathy chairs. Berthet gestured him to one of the chairs and sat down in the other.

"You used to run a lab, didn't you?" Berthet said, smiling, which seemed beside the point.

"I made sure Louis Dalloz's books balanced," he said.

"More than that, I heard. So let me ask you. Suppose you have a very talented man who shows up with injuries—"

"Just a dog bite. Boring."

"—*Unexplained* injuries, but no doubt painful, and the man is feeling under pressure to prove a very interesting theory, and his scope's been stolen. What would you tell him?"

Berthet beamed at him: encouraging the pupil to come up with a good answer. Berthet was a smallish man with a big smile and the rural accent of southern France. He wore glasses and had his hair cut in a silly fringe like a medieval monk. He twinkled. Under it all was a vastly intelligent thinker and psychologist, who knew exactly how to be reassuring. It still worked.

"I'd tell him to get organized."

"Organization first. The theory will keep, just a little," Berthet said. "You know it will. How is your arm? Are you doing what the doctor tells you?"

"Almost," he admitted.

"Exercise; your muscles will stiffen if you don't. I know you're working; tell me what you're doing."

He was on clearer ground there and gave a summary; Berthet seemed satisfied.

"Your microscope. If it's not found, have you thought of switching to the Zeiss ultraviolet scope?" The Zeiss UV scope was a very new thing, and reportedly more trouble than it was worth. "Have you looked at it?"

"No. Where I am now, it'd be a distraction, don't you think?"

"Perhaps you need a distraction," Berthet suggested.

Reisden raised an eyebrow.

Berthet leaned forward, grinning. "When I made my first breakthrough, about your age, I had to sit down and write articles about it. I couldn't do it. I was so impressed with the importance of what I had to do— It was like being told 'you have to take a shit now,' you try and you try and nothing works, eh? Much better to take a good walk and let things happen naturally. There, now, you're laughing. This thing with Jouvet, it may not be so bad for you."

"Jouvet is a distraction. My cousin asked me to do it and I shouldn't have. I'm sorry."

"I hear from Louis that you have a head for business and you do things like that. We'll have you on the finance committee." Berthet sobered. "Poor Jules. I knew him very well; I hoped we'd have him forever. It's time for the company to go, I suppose, but he got together a fine group of people.

Some of them will need help to move forward. Will you do that?"

Not what he'd expected. "What I can do, I will."

"I think you will. You're a compassionate man."

"Oh, G-d, I am not!" he said, startled.

"Especially Mme Herschner. She's remarkable, and she'll never again have the opportunities she had under Jules. I wish I could hire her myself. Meanwhile, you can do a little job for me. There's a man you should connect with, Paul Polin. He does ultramicroscopic work too; get him to tell you about it. I want you two to look at the Zeiss UV, report to me, and if it's worth while, work on a plan to get it funded for the lab. Take Polin to dinner. He's shy."

❧

He left, somewhat encouraged; gently rebuked; surprised. Berthet was apparently undisturbed by his being involved in Jouvet. *Take care of the people;* particularly, it seemed, of Mme Herschner.

Compassionate? No.

He headed for the lab front desk to get his mail and leave a message for Polin: no use putting that off.

"Monsieur le docteur, Monsieur de Reisden!" The porter waved at him as he approached. "The police called. They've found your microscope!"

❧

It was barely an hour before the lost property office closed. He took a taxi, arrived just in time to talk himself in, spent the next half hour dealing with French paperwork and convincing the Préfecture that the scope was really his, and getting one passionate look at it before the office closed. He emerged with it into a driving rain. He wanted to take it to a café and look it over and wine and dine it, but restrained himself; still he kept one hand on it all the long ride back to the lab. The scope had been double-packed, its own box inside a shipping crate padded with crushed newspaper. Now the shipping crate was gone and the fitted mahogany box was mauled, split, and dented inward.

He wouldn't know anything until he'd checked.

At his bench, he moved everything carefully aside, positioned his lights, unlocked the box, and lifted the base and body of the scope onto the bench. It relieved him, in a deep obscure way, just to feel its big familiar weight. "Come, my dear, let's check you out." He tipped each objective carefully out of its box and screwed them into the nosepiece—no damage visible—and turned the coarse focus to raise the body so he could screw the nosepiece in.

Something was wrong. The body moved reluctantly, hitching and loose.

"No. *Fuck* no."

He shone one of the lights at the rack and cleaned the screw and rack mechanism. The head felt wobbly and the coarse focus slipped and grabbed. The fine focus didn't move at all. He put the detergent and alcohol and cloth back, came back to the bench and stared at his broken microscope, slammed his hand against the side of the cabinet, and cursed comprehensively. Himself, the thief, the railroad security system, himself again.

"Hello?"

Somebody at the lab door, hesitating shyly.

"What?" Reisden snapped.

"I'm…Polin?"

It would be Polin, of course, exactly now.

Polin came out into the light, blinking behind his glasses. He looked like an intelligent snail, as if he'd shrink from being touched. He was at least half Chinese, which was a surprise.

"Sorry," Reisden said. He was supposed to be nice to Polin. He didn't have it in him. "I just got my scope back and it's comprehensively broken. I am really sorry. Come back tomorrow. No. I'll find you. Where's your bench?"

"Room 4," Polin whispered.

"No. Wait." The man worked with an ultramicroscope too. "Where should I have my scope repaired?"

"Allard's."

He took it back to the apartment at Jouvet for the night. This was sentiment and self-pity; it wasn't going to get stolen from Physio.Psych. He spent far too much time setting it up on Dr. Jouvet's work desk and examining it with the best lamp the apartment provided, cleaning the coarse focus adjustment again as if somehow it would relent and repair itself; but he could see the scoring across the rack.

The next morning, he took it to Allard's. Even in the rain, the shelves of brass instruments glittered and gleamed. "I've brought this to be repaired."

And the repair clerk scorned him.

French repairmen prefer to work on French instruments, the clerk at Allard's implied. He was a smug man with an offensively waxed moustache. They'd do Zeiss, of course, because Zeiss is Zeiss, but Bausch & Lomb? An *American* company? His instrument got respect for being a Grand Continental, but you understand, monsieur, why would one stock *American* parts? It would be possible to order the focusing rack from New York, yes; one could attempt to install it, but…

Allard's clearly didn't want to take it on.

He could have the parts custom-milled by a man in Switzerland, which would mean going to Switzerland because he wasn't going to abandon his scope again. He could attempt to have the parts milled in Paris, which would put him at the mercy of whoever did it, or order Bausch & Lomb parts from New York.

(He'd *been* in New York two months ago.

(Perdita was in New York. He could go again. It would be natural to drop in on her—

(*No.*)

Whatever he did, it would take weeks. *Merde.*

"I'll order the parts; will you try it?"

"We'll put you on the waiting list, monsieur."

Organization. He jotted a list in his pocket notebook. Get the parts for the scope. Vet the whole scope; identifying one problem didn't mean there weren't others. Talk to the insurers. Look willing for Berthet and look at the Zeiss UV scope. Take Polin.

He took Polin to lunch. Polin was Indochinese, not Chinese; he called himself Vietnamese. They talked about Vietnamese politics and the weather (it was still raining heavily). November, Reisden quoted cautiously, when the English jump off bridges. Polin replied equally cautiously that the Buddha said suicide was a negative act and should be avoided. "The Buddha is right," Reisden said emphatically. They seemed to have said anything that needed said.

They went to the Zeiss showroom and were given a demonstration of the UX, a huge camera almost swallowing a high-end scope like a serpent swallowing a sepoy. One looked at everything on a phosphor screen. Reisden tried it with his test slides.

"Good detail. And I don't like it," he said.

"It is not intimate," Polin agreed. "One doesn't feel connected."

"Right. That screen."

"Green as the flag of Nejd."

"And I don't fancy losing my sight and glowing purple, using it."

"A blind man, giving light," Polin agreed.

Reisden decided Polin was interesting.

᎒

He went off to beg tea from Dotty. She wasn't there, so he spent some time improving his acquaintance with Tiggy. Tiggy actually smiled at him and consented to be read to.

He showed Tiggy how to spin a top. "Wind the string like this." Tiggy, being three, made a mare's nest of it. Reisden showed him again.

If Rose Rossi's son were still alive, she would have been teaching her boy how to wind string around a top instead of buying toys for orphans.

Thirty-six tops, sixteen block sets, twenty-one bears...

What would Tiggy like for Christmas?

Perhaps the intended recipient should have a say. Years ago in Paris, the big department stores had decorated their windows with moving figures. Did they still?

"Would you like to see the windows at the *grands magasins* once they're up?"

Tiggy nodded solemnly.

᎒

He ate out, *steack et frites* in a smoky restaurant full of shouting students and an accordion player playing "La Maxixe", and came back to do another round of brooding over his microscope. Instead, he found Mme Herschner waiting for him with her plan to prove Rose Rossi innocent.

"We'll have her speak with someone. Someone *très sympathique,* a consultant of ours, Lucie Ray. You've met her. She wears a veil."

The elderly woman, veiled, in the fashionable red dress; she'd been at Jouvet the first night.

"You should see—" Mme Herschner stood up. "Wait a minute."

It was several minutes before she came back with a folder. She riffled through it, and came out with a carte de visite, a palm-sized photograph of a pretty, flirtatious girl in the curls of the 1860s. There was her name under it, Lucie Ray, and a line of text: *C'était moi. This was me.*

"She was one of our patients just after I first came here," Mme Herschner said. "Look at her face. Look until you'd recognize her."

He nodded.

"Now," she opened the folder again and handed him a second photo. "Do you recognize her still?"

He sucked in his breath.

"Do you recognize her?" Mme Herschner repeated.

He looked back and forth between the two photographs. "Yes," he said finally.

"Lucie is one of the bravest people I know," Mme Herschner said. "She was caught in a fire during the siege. She came to us; she said *I cannot bear to be without my face.*

She talked and talked with Dr. Jouvet, and then she came up with that herself."

Mme Herschner smiled. Her plain face transformed.

"She started giving out pictures of her old self so that people could see the face beyond the scars."

"She *drew attention* to her face," he said.

She looked up at him, her face still glowing. "She says she's never had a superficial friend since."

"And she'd do—what—for Rose Rossi?"

"She'll let Rose know she's not alone."

"But if Rose is guilty," he said. He'd been thinking of it. What she would have felt afterward, when it was too late.

"Some people, Madame Herschner; some people do something so wrong they never get free. Whatever the state of her face is, if she murdered her child, what about that? What can you do? What can anyone do?"

These were clearly not ideas he should have if he meant to be a normal person.

"She still needs our help. We're not here just for the innocent."

❧

Lucie Ray herself appeared late the next afternoon. It was still raining, a soaking, persistent November rain. He'd taken the microscope down to the Jouvet lab floor, for the sake of the electric light, and was checking it out again at one of the unused benches. Nothing else wrong with it as far as he could tell; but could he tell?

"Monsieur le docteur? Lucie Ray is here."

He followed Mme Herschner upstairs and into Dr. Jouvet's office, where Lucie Ray was shaking out her wet skirts by the fire. "Eve, what an afternoon. Is there tea? Honestly. There had better be tea."

Her wet veil was clinging over her face. She peeled it back. He forced himself not to look away. Then she took off her hat.

Then she took off her hair.

He didn't look away. He looked at the red, ropy scars, the waxy patches of hairless skin, the lipless mouth; and then she tilted her head on one side and smiled at him, and he saw the face beyond the face the fire had left her.

"Welcome, Madame Ray. Thank you for coming to help."

"It's my pleasure. I only hope I can do something."

Mme Herschner brought tea: British crumpets, butter, jam, cheese. He toasted crumpets over the gas fire for them all and listened while the women sat in the two Dr. Jouvet sympathy chairs and planned. "She goes only to the Paradis for toys, the Samaritaine for children's clothes, and her esthetician," Mme Herschner said. "Every two or three days for the esthetician."

"Who is this esthetician?" Lucie Ray asked. Mme Herschner gave a name. "That one doesn't know anything about burns."

"Her mother's esthetician," Mme Herschner said, shrugging.

"That won't do at all, Eve."

"My cousin says Rose Rossi wouldn't use an esthetician if she were badly scarred," Reisden offered.

Lucie Ray shook her head. "She would have to use someone. Scar tissue is difficult, especially in the first few years. One needs to exercise, one gets massages, herbal baths, I grease my poor face like a pig, and as for the summers, it's no joke not sweating. Eve, this jam is magnificent; did you make it?"

"I did."

"I'm taking my pay in jam. How do you think I should approach her?"

"I leave that to you."

"No, you can't this time. I'm not sure I'm the right person for this." Lucie Ray stood up, dusting crumbs off her skirt. She had taken the chair farther from the fire. She stood with the chair between the fire and herself. He had a sense of her: not afraid perhaps, but always careful. "Think, Eve. I come up to her on the street, at night, outside her esthetician's perhaps. She's all alone. It's dark, I say I've read about her in the papers, I believe her story, and perhaps I can help. And then," she lifted an invisible veil, "I take off my veil. And she screams. She may be used to her face; but to mine?"

She let her scarred hands fall against the back of the chair. "When I talk to people for you, they're ready to look at me and ask questions. But is she ready?" She came round the side of the chair again and dropped into it. "Remember how long it took me."

"There isn't time, Lucie," Mme Herschner said. "I told you. *Eleven days* left." Both women looked at him.

"Yes," he said. "Eleven days left."

"Then of course I'll try. But I'll be too matter-of-fact for her, talking about Chinese herbs and skin creams and such. I'm not *sympa.*"

"She doesn't even go to Mass," Mme Herschner said. "Or have a priest come to her house. She doesn't make confession, she hasn't since *then.* She has to talk to someone."

"Do you think she's guilty?" Reisden asked Lucie Ray.

Lucie Ray gave a long sigh. "Guilty... When one looks different and people treat one badly because of it, one can feel something like guilt, you know? But—" She touched her wedding ring. "If she killed her son—" She pressed her hands against her eyelashless eyelids for a moment. "I'm repelled by what she might have done to her child, monsieur. But if she veiled herself and pretended to be burned as an alibi, you would think I'd be repelled by that, but I feel sad for her. Terrified for her. She couldn't have known what it would do to her. She's alone behind that veil. Guilty or not, we have to get her out."

The two women sat in a thick silence. The gas fire hissed in the grate. A toast-crumb caught in the flame and flared. If she's guilty, Reisden thought. I know what it's like to be alone with it afterward. And what it's like to talk about it, finally. To nerve yourself up to, to be forced to, to find a way to talk.

Last summer, he'd found Gilbert and Perdita to talk to.

If she had done it, she was where he'd been.

Not a place to be.

"How soon can we talk to her?" Lucie Ray asked.

"The next time she goes out to her esthetician," Mme Herschner said. "She goes every two or three days."

"She won't go until after the rain stops." Lucie held up her veil and flapped it damply. "Have you ever tried breathing through a wet veil? And she wears a mask as well."

"We'll watch," Mme Herschner said. "I'll telephone you when she goes out."

"I'll be at my daughter's. Poor Bertrand, my husband will be a bachelor until this is over. He adores your jam, you know."

"I'll send him a case."

"Some of your paradise jelly? But not too much. He could eat it with a spoon." Lucie Ray fit her wig over her head. For a moment, with the ordinary hair next to her face, she was hideous again. He realized how quickly he'd got used to the face she had. She pinned on her hat and her veil clung around her face. "Ugh. Definitely, she won't go out until after the rain."

ᕀ

Until after the rain... Every evening, coming back from Physio.Psych. or from Dotty's, Reisden would see Mme Herschner waiting at her secretary's desk outside Dr. Jouvet's office until nine o'clock, ten o'clock every night. Waiting for news. Waiting for the rain to stop gurgling in the gutters.

He'd stop; they'd look at each other.

"No word?" he'd ask.

"She *is* innocent," she'd say, "she only needs to talk," and he didn't know whether she simply hoped it.

So Mme Herschner waited, and he watched her waiting. The rain sheeted down windows and hammered the surface of the Seine. Rain thrummed on umbrellas and women hurried into doorways, their skirts clinging around their boots. The Eiffel Tower was only a dim halo in the clouds. Condensation fogged the eyepieces in the Physio.Psych. lab., where he looked through a bad scope and saw nothing.

"Have you had dinner?" he asked Mme Herschner one night. He went out again for bread and market oysters from the rue de Buci for them both, and came back in time to see a squelching homeless man reporting to Mme Herschner that, once again, Rose Rossi hadn't left her house.

"Come in by the fire," he said, and lit the gas-log in Dr. Jouvet's office. He pulled the two sympathy chairs next to it and gestured her to take one of them. He stretched out his legs by the fire. His trousers steamed and smelled of wool.

"It'll stop raining soon," she said.

He opened an oyster with his penknife and handed it to her.

She went into the food cupboard in the techs' room and came back with a bread knife, butter, towels for their fingers, and a half jar of rose-pink jam. She made an oyster sandwich for herself: oyster, bread, butter. She dabbed a tiny dollop of the jam on top of an oyster.

"Really?" he said.

"Try it."

He tried jam on the corner of an oyster, on the principle one should try anything once. Sweet, citrusy, not entirely bad.

"How did you come to work for Dr. Jouvet?" he asked.

She was sitting in the patient's chair; he was in Dr. Jouvet's. *Tell me everything*— She squared her shoulders, clasped her hands, and looked down at her knuckles.

"It was the winter of the siege and the commune," she said. "I had married a German man, a violinist in a cafe. Hans went home when the war started and died fighting us. I loved Hans, but he was *stupid* about the war, he didn't want to fight but he went—" She looked up, her young self shadowing her face. "We were being shelled all the time. The bombs shook the buildings. People were dying on the barricades, in the streets, of starvation, of wounds. It was spring but all the trees had been cut down, all the flower bulbs had been dug up for eating.

"People were going mad from terror."

She stopped for a moment. "*Mad* from terror. From sadness. From not knowing what would happen next. The constant uncertainty. I saw Dr. Jouvet on the streets, dressing wounds, and then I saw him sitting on a park bench listening to a woman whose house had been bombed. She didn't know anything, she didn't know what would happen for the rest of her life— I asked if I could help and I've never left." She ate a second oyster sandwich and wiped her fingers fastidiously. "Poverty, uncertainty, they don't frighten me, monsieur. What frightens me is not helping. How did you become a chemist?"

"The right tutor when I was sixteen. He said chemistry would explain everything."

"Do you want to explain everything, monsieur le docteur?"

"Of course. Do you want to help everyone?"

"Yes. Rose Rossi first." She looked out the window at the rain, relentlessly falling, then back at him, and visibly nerved herself. He thought she'd ask about keeping Jouvet open past next Thursday. But—

"Did chemistry help you, monsieur? In your trouble?"

Of course she knew his history, or thought she knew.

"It was the only thing that did," he said soberly.

No. He owed it to Gilbert and Perdita, here in Dr. Jouvet's office where so many secrets had come out. "I met—two people. They brought me—I don't know. What did you say? Back into the world?"

"How?" she asked professionally.

"No way that would help Rose Rossi."

She didn't move, just sat attentively. He opened another oyster. The knife slipped and he nicked the base of his thumb, not badly, but it stung and bled. She got up and found a sticking-plaster. He held out his hand while she put it on.

"I was a foundling," he said. "That sounds Dickensian; it really wasn't bad. Dotty's father brought me into their family when I was nine or ten. But I met my real uncle last summer. That did explain everything; not everything, enough. And there was a friend of the family, a girl—" He broke off.

"You liked her," Mme Herschner guessed.

"I liked them both."

"So you talk with them now?"

He shook his head. "I know who I am. Not Gilbert's nephew."

"But you write each other at least."

"Best not."

"But you know they're there."

Oh, yes, they're there. Perdita's at the piano in Dr. Jouvet's apartment. "I have my cousin Dotty and her son," he said. "They're enough. Do you have family?"

"Not any more. They didn't like my marrying Hans."

"After thirty-five years?" he said. "Surely—"

"The Germans still have Alsace, monsieur, and my family still hates the Germans. I have my family here at Jouvet."

Had, he thought silently. Had.

"If only Rose would talk to someone!" Mme Herschner said. "Anyone."

"Who?"

"Someone who would just listen."

∽

Someone who would listen. What would that listener hear?

He walked up to the Gare d'Orsay in the rain and watched the trains leaving for Switzerland. The rain swished over the glass station roof and the trains chuffed hollowly off into the tunnels, going somewhere else. In Switzerland the rain would be snow. He could go back to Switzerland with his scope. He could go back, and leave Paris; go back to doing all his lab work alone and never speak to anyone again.

Like Rose Rossi behind her veil.

I will not leave, he said to himself. *I will not leave.*

It rained all weekend and into the next week, while Mme Herschner looked with increasing desperation out the window. Jouvet would close. Mme Herschner was about to lose her place, her family. Reisden lay awake at night in Dr. Jouvet's apartment, knowing how a guilty person feels, and just wanting to feel normal, whatever that was, and not care who Rose Rossi talked to or didn't.

But, with two days to go until the end of Jouvet, he made an appointment with Rose Rossi's father.

∽

"What are you doing for my daughter, eh?"

The owner of Rossi's Fine Groceries—unless Mathilde de St.-Martin owned it—lived in an elegant *hôtel particulier* in Neuilly, near the Bois de Boulogne. It was large enough to have two wings, a garden, and a greenhouse. Charles Rossi received him in the greenhouse, which was warm and steaming with damp. Rose Rossi's father was a short, stout, grey-blond man in shirtsleeves, red-faced and cylindrical as his own red-labeled cans. His hair stood up in exclamation marks. He was looking up at a grove of banana trees, their leaves almost as long as he was tall.

Reisden explained the situation as honestly as he could. Jouvet was closing; they were doing what they could.

"But you're not keeping Jouvet going."

"No."

"Well, I hired Jouvet; so what are you going to do about that?"

This much he could do. "I have a suggestion for you, something that may truly help your daughter. Dr. Jouvet's assistant was with him for thirty-five years. She knows his procedures and his experts, and she's entirely devoted to proving your daughter's innocence. When Jouvet closes, Mme Herschner will lose her place. Would you hire her to talk with your daughter?"

Rossi stuck out his lower lip. "Some old woman?"

"Without Dr. Jouvet, she's the closest there is to Jouvet. And a woman will be better to talk with your daughter than any man."

"Any man except Dr. Jouvet."

"We'd all like him here."

"I should ask for my money back."

"I don't want to give it." Rossi looked a little surprised; he'd expected a gentleman's *of course I will.* "I'll do it if you insist, but we both want to help your daughter."

Rossi crossed his arms and looked at Reisden. Reisden looked back.

"Come with me," Rossi said. "This is what your Mme Herschner would have to deal with."

Rossi led him out of the greenhouse, down a long corridor lined with elaborate, deserted rooms. One door was stubbornly closed. "That leads to her rooms," Rossi said. "She goes out by a separate entrance. I have a key, but—" He shrugged. "I want her to come out. Can your Mme Herschner get her to come out?"

"Back into the world? She'll try."

Rossi kept going until they reached the center of the house, a grand entrance hall, icy white marble. The only color in the room was a huge portrait of a beautiful girl, a blonde butterfly in silk and diamonds, smiling and showing off the blaze of her engagement ring. She was shockingly young, a schoolgirl. Sixteen. *Sixteen,* and went to the Congo with a psychopath.

"That's what I want for her," Rose's father said. "To be like that again. Can your Mme Herschner give her that?"

"No."

"I want her to be happy. I want a man to love her. I want her to have children; I want grandchildren. I want her to trust me enough to come out of her rooms and speak to me… speak to me… I haven't heard my child's voice since she came back from Africa, do you know that? She writes me. *Writes.* She was a brave, strong girl, and now… Can your Mme Herschner give me that?"

"Perhaps." He hadn't missed the change from *give her* to *give me.*

"I want her to know," Rossi said. "Whatever she looks like, whatever she looks like, she'll be my daughter. Dr. Jouvet gave me a picture to look at. A burned woman." His voice went thick. "*Whatever* she looks like."

And whatever she had done to Philippe?

He asked.

"Do you believe the rumors about her?"

Charles Rossi looked up at him sharply. "She's innocent."

"She may not be."

"No. You don't understand. Whatever she did, she is innocent. She was seventeen. She's barely twenty now. I believe in her innocence. No matter what she did. I *know* that she did not kill her son."

"But you think she killed Godefroy," Reisden said, suddenly understanding.

ȣ

"It was my fault," Rossi said. "I was greedy for her. To be a duchess! My daughter! A duchess and a diplomat's wife! *My* daughter! *I* put her there, with that man. —I think that she is innocent in spirit." The little grocer looked up at his daughter's portrait. "Whatever she has done. But whatever she looks like, whatever she says to me, *whatever she has done*, I want to see her face and hear her voice. She is my *daughter.*"

"There are murders—" Reisden started to say, and caught himself. Murders that can be forgiven by everyone but the person who did them. Godefroy, perhaps. Not Philippe. Never. Forgivable by no one. "Mme Herschner will do her best for your daughter."

Rossi sniffed roughly. "Promise me," he said. "*You* promise me *yourself*, that this Mme Herschner —"

"I do promise you."

"Then I'll see her. Hire her, if she's any good. Wait. Don't go yet. Come back to the greenhouse a moment."

Rossi led the way back through the cold corridors into the warm greenhouse. He looked up among the huge leaves of the banana trees. A few bananas, hidden: he dragged a ladder over, climbed up, considered, and picked two. "One for this Mme Herschner. One for you. They're never so good as when they're just picked."

In the cab going back to Jouvet, he stared at the bananas, hands shaking. He had almost talked about murder to Charles Rossi.

I think that she is innocent in spirit? That much he knew: there's no such thing.

⪍

Thursday, the last day of Jouvet. The forecast called for clearing, but the forecast was wrong; it rained steadily all the morning, ticking against the windows of Physio.Psych. *I told her I wouldn't keep Jouvet open,* Reisden reminded himself. *I've done what I can.*

It wasn't enough.

He'd drive himself crazy and he couldn't do that.

He needed distraction. The replacement scope parts had arrived, remarkably promptly, from Bausch & Lomb in New York. He telephoned Allard's to see if they'd move his microscope up the queue. No.

He went off to talk with Paul Polin about the Zeiss UV scope, but Polin was in the middle of an experiment and couldn't be disturbed.

He decided to inflict himself on Dotty for tea.

And even she wasn't home; she was at some pre-Christmas charity bazaar. He went up to see Tiggy. Tiggy was bored too and clearly hoped Uncle Sacha had come to entertain him.

"Shall we go see the Christmas windows?"

"But, monsieur, it's raining!" the nursemaid objected.

"It has always rained; it will always rain."

They left the nursemaid and, at Tiggy's insistence, they took the horse-car. Tiggy adored the horse-car, the polished brass, the zinging bell, the smell of damp leather seats and warm animals, the ticket-taker with his round cap, above all the driver magnificently conducting the horses like a maestro at the Opera. Tiggy insisted on sitting at the front to watch. *Philippe was Tiggy's age,* Reisden thought, watching him. They toured the Christmas windows with their dancing marionette-figures, which impressed Tiggy less than the horse-cars, and then went to the Paradis des enfants, where Reisden tried to deduce what Tiggy wanted for Christmas.

It was packed with parents shopping for presents. He put Tiggy up on his shoulders—his arm, surprisingly, didn't hurt; he must be getting better—and they toured the toys. Tiggy considered the Steiff stuffed animals and dolls: a Dutch boy, a clown, an army officer, a conductor-like policeman. Reisden asked Tiggy "Do you like the conductor-doll?" and was told sternly that the conductor was not a *doll* but a *personnage.* Boys didn't play with *dolls.*

Then Tiggy found the model trucks and cars. Reisden let him down and he went straight for the model horse-car. Two horses in front, a driver *personnage,* and passengers lithographed in the windows. Clearly the proper thing for Christmas. Reisden dealt quietly with the sales clerk while Tiggy played.

Rose Rossi had bought gifts for children. Why?

Had she killed her own child?

Killed her husband?

Or was she innocent?

He had the kind of mind that numbers cling to. She'd bought twenty-one bears, sixteen sets of blocks, thirty-six spinning tops, fifteen dolls. While he watched Tiggy, he made number patterns. All but the 16, a multiple of 3; all but the 15, multiple of 5 + 1. Middle two, squares. Proving that the mind likes patterns.

Proving that he'd rather think about anything than Rose Rossi.

Tiggy was yawning. "Shall we go home?" Reisden suggested.

But Tiggy wanted to buy a present. "It's *very* important," he said. "It's *for* someone."

"For your mother?" Reisden guessed. Tiggy shook his head solemnly. *For your father?* he didn't ask. He wouldn't ask Tiggy what Dotty wouldn't tell him.

Tiggy laid his little hand gravely on the very smallest of the Steiff bears, a palm-sized Teddy with a red ribbon around its neck. "This one."

"A good choice."

For whom? Tiggy was too small to go to school. He must have some particular friend.

∞

They went back to Dotty's by taxi. By the time they reached the place Dauphine, Tiggy was asleep. Reisden left him with the nursemaid and went to find Dotty, meaning to get invited to dinner.

She was standing in the hall, still in her wet outdoor coat. She turned to face him, waving a telegraph form. "From Brazzaville, darling!"

And in her horrified, delighted smile, he saw Rose Rossi was guilty.

❧

Mme Herschner was sitting at her usual place, at her secretarial desk, waiting for the rain to stop. "Come into the office," he said. She lit the gas fire while he took off his wet coat. They sat in the sympathy chairs and he silently passed her Sigi's telegram.

Sigi had been thorough; he'd gone upriver with a friend in the river police to investigate. Rose had been a favorite at the trading post. The villagers had defended her universally, with precisely similar stories, had said in a well-trained chorus that Philippe had died in the fire.

ALL LYING, Sigi had telegraphed.

Sigi had gone to the next village, where a woman had said Philippe had been badly burned, but was alive the next day.

Sigi had added, in code, that apparently Godefroy had tortured several of the village women; so the village had supported Rose's story.

Mathilde is right! Dotty had said. *Rose killed him! Oh, darling, isn't it awful.*

He watched Mme Herschner while she read the telegram and the animation went out of her face. The gas fire hissed and popped as rain came down the chimney.

"The poor woman," she said.

"Oh? At the very least, she said Godefroy killed the boy and lied about his death afterward. At the worst, he survived and she killed him.—For a share in a *grocery business.* She killed a *child.*"

"Have you ever talked with a murderer?" Mme Herschner asked.

Yes. No. "My nephew is three years old. I've only just met him, and if anyone *used* him as she must have—"

"There's a kind of merciful forgetting sometimes," Mme Herschner said. "Among people who have killed. She was burned herself, it hurts terribly, perhaps she didn't know what to do. Monsieur, they don't believe they could have done it. They get confused. They remember almost up until the moment, and then they say 'And something happened.'"

"A *merciful* forgetting?"

"She might not even be *sure* whether she killed him. She might simply have—" Mme Herschner held out her hands as if she were pushing something away.

She saw his expression and misunderstood it.

"It happens, monsieur. 'Something' happens."

"Forgetting is not merciful," he said. "Don't call it merciful, ever. Because no matter how you try to escape, what you do waits for you."

He must have been too emphatic. She moved a little back in the chair.

"I'm sorry," he said.

The fire clicked and ticked between them.

"We can help," she said. "While she remembers."

"You may not have heard this," he said. "When I —" he made a gesture. "Before I—" He tried again. "My wife died in a car accident. I was driving. I thought I meant to do it. I couldn't be convinced otherwise. Everyone kept telling me I wasn't to blame. I *knew* I was."

She nodded, listening.

He added quickly, "I was wrong, but I knew it. The one thing worse, I think, would be not being sure. Not knowing. Not remembering, not having anything but the guilt. Don't call it merciful."

"Then you understand," she said.

"I don't. She didn't forget. He lived past the fire, and then he died, and she lied about it. She didn't forget. She just d—n lied."

Neither of them said anything for a moment.

"And you intend to help her face it?" he said. "That isn't merciful either."

"I can't bear it that no one will help her," Mme Herschner said.

"You are probably a saint. G-d forgive you."

It was time to talk with Mme Herschner about her own future.

"I arranged a chance for you. That was before we knew," he indicated the telegram. "Charles Rossi will hire you to talk with her if you pass his muster, which you will. Do you still want to?"

"Yes," she said.

"In spite of—? Why?"

"It's my job."

Jouvet would cease to exist at midnight, but Mme Herschner would always be a part of Jouvet. Her family. Her lifelong job.

"You could do something different with your life," he said. Giving her a chance to get out of it.

"Would you still do chemistry, monsieur, if you knew you would never, never find a new fact?"

"Yes."

"Why?"

"'Never, never' could be wrong."

"And even if it isn't."

"I'd do my best to make it wrong."

"There you are," she said.

"You can't make her innocent."

"Forgiven."

"Not by me. —I'll tell Charles Rossi."

"What will you do?" she said. "After this? When Jouvet is—?"

"Move out of here, get my microscope back, cut up frogs."

"Every time you come by this building," she said, "you'll think 'Jouvet could have been here.'"

"That's you, Mme Herschner. Not me."

She sighed. "We should have—" She stopped. What should *we* have done? "Well, then, I hope Allard's finishes with your microscope soon and you enjoy your frogs." She was trying not to say anything bitter, clearly. He was closing down what had been her family and her life.

"Who's doing the work on your scope?" she asked, changing the subject, businesslike. "Some of his techs are better than others."

"I don't know yet," he said. "Who should I ask for?"

"But," she said. "No— Allard's didn't put you on the *wait list?*"

He shrugged.

"But you're from Jouvet."

"I'm not from Jouvet."

"But *you* don't get put on the *wait list*. Excuse me a moment."

She left the door open as she telephoned from her desk. "Good evening, Monsieur Georges," he heard her saying. The conversation went on for almost ten minutes, the last minutes of Jouvet's life ticking past. She came back into the room.

"Go see Monsieur Allard tomorrow. Bring your instrument and the parts. He says a week at most."

"Georges Allard," he said. "That was Georges Allard you spoke with?"

"He's an old friend of Jouvet."

She had talked with Allard like an equal. "Thank you." It was almost shocking relief. A week. In a week he'd get his scope back and he could see again. Be himself again. Never have to face anyone locked alone behind a veil, trying to be unseen even to themselves.

"You're welcome, monsieur." She used his name for the first time. "Monsieur de Reisden."

"Madame Herschner."

They'd said everything they needed to, and the conversation could have ended, but he stayed by the fire and so did she, both of them silent. He thought of Berthet commending her to him. *Mme Herschner, a remarkable woman, and she'll never again have the opportunity she had under Jules.*

"Look," he said. "Go ahead, try to be merciful to Rose Rossi. If you can. But afterward? Jouvet's was extraordinary. But it was wrong. A single great man and his minions, that's not how a modern lab works, even when there is a great man. Labs run on administration and committees. You're good at administration and you'll always be needed. Don't sell yourself short. Don't tie yourself to one guilty woman. Find a lab to run."

"But I want *this* lab," she said.

"The lab is nothing without Dr. Jouvet," he said.

And finally, finally, he listened to what he was saying; listened to what he and everyone else in Paris had said about Jouvet.

Jouvet is nothing without Dr. Jouvet.

In Dr. Jouvet's office, medical textbooks thirty years out of date. In Dr. Jouvet's apartment, unanswered letters, unopened piles of books; the chaos of a life that had got too big for one old man.

He had said it himself. Jouvet didn't look like a company run by a near-centenarian.

A single great man didn't run a lab.

Administrators did.

Oh, he thought. Oh.

"You ran Jouvet?" he said.

"We all did," she said. "We all do."

∽

"How long," he asked, "since Dr. Jouvet was actually leading this lab?"

She raised her head, half proudly, half defensively. "Ten years?"

"Ten years?"

"He had a stroke in 1895."

Eleven years. Almost twelve.

"But he still came out on occasion. He was perfectly lucid but— When he— We would say, *he's not feeling well today, would you mind seeing someone else? Dr. Jouvet has thoroughly briefed this expert. Dr. Jouvet recommends you see this specialist...* And our patients didn't mind because Dr. Jouvet had told them what to do. *Oh yes,* they said, *Dr. Jouvet helped.* We were good. We *are* good. We know how to listen, monsieur; he taught us. We're a fine lab; he made us. But—

"It was our fault, we built him up, we kept hiding behind him, no one saw the rest of us, no one saw what we could do. And when he died, it was *Jouvet's just another lab without him.*"

Reisden had said that himself, though he knew differently.

"I want us to *survive.* Survive and keep helping."

"And you think you could do it," he said.

"No," she said. "No one believes in magic without a magician. We needed Dr. Jouvet," she said. "I don't think we can, us staff, all by ourselves."

He looked at her: short, plain, greying, in her mourning dress and her matronly cameo. The sixth Dr. Jouvet. One of them. One of them, with the lab techs, with the experts, with Lucie Ray. With the files, with the building, with all of them ready to go on unseen.

No one would believe her.

"Hire a magician."

"We need a real doctor with a real degree," she said.

And a building. And the archives.

Someone who'd administered a lab. As he'd administered Louis Dalloz's lab. Someone with a nice shiny Ph.D. and a connection to the Physio.Psych. lab. With an aura of scientific respectability. Someone with enough money to start it back up. Someone normal. More or less.

She'd wanted him to take over the company.

"Not me," he said. "I don't do anything like that. I cut up frogs."

"Let us *try,*" she said. "You don't have to do anything. All you have to do is not shut us down and let us *try.*"

Jouvet could have helped me, he'd said to Fourche. At Physio.Psych., half the men still looked at him sideways. He wouldn't say yes. It wasn't his job, it wasn't his responsibility, he didn't want it, he wouldn't do it. It would brand him forever. The madman who owned the madhouse.

"The h—l with the rain," he said. "Let's break into her house."

Her head jerked up. "Us, monsieur?"

"I don't mean *break in,* I mean— Yes. Corner her in her house. Her father has the keys. You, Lucie Ray, me. If she won't talk, make her listen."

"Yes, but—" Mme Herschner gestured at the telegram.

"Lucie Ray can talk with her about the burning. For the rest," he said—

What can a murderer say to a murderer? How much can a murderer bear to hear?

He didn't know. He didn't want to.

"You are not going to tell anyone this," he said. "Never. Anyone. Do you understand? But you may hear something tonight and you shouldn't be surprised by it. I told you I thought I'd murdered my wife. I was lying. I thought I'd murdered her because I did murder someone else. Yes, one can get confused. No, it isn't merciful. At all. I owe someone something. I'll listen to her tonight."

He felt as though he'd torn away his own face. She simply looked up at him and nodded once, as if she'd recognized him. He wondered bleakly, do other people see that, do they sense it? A murderer? Is that who I really am?

Yes.

He was never going to be normal. Never ordinary.

"I don't know whether I can do this. She *killed a child.* I don't know that I can listen to that. All I know—" He took a deep breath. "All I know is it's death to be alone with it. Let's go."

The rain stopped when their taxi was halfway to the Rossi house in Neuilly. They looked at each other.

"God wants us to do this," Mme Herschner said.

Lucie Ray was waiting for them in front of the Rossi house. "She's left," she said. "She's going to her esthetician."

Their taxi actually passed Rose Rossi on the boulevard. She was limping down the street, a black haunt under the streetlights, and people shrank from her. They found seats on the *terrasse* of a café opposite the beauty parlor and watched as she arrived. The beauty parlor had already darkened its windows, but Rose knocked on the door and it opened.

"We wait for her to leave," Mme Herschner said, "and talk to her on the street."

"Not on the street, dear," Lucie Ray said. "We'll find a nice quiet place where she can cry."

Reisden leaned forward as the beauty parlor door opened again, but it was only a laundress, a young woman in a plain coat and wide hat, head down, pushing a wheeled wicker laundry basket. He watched idly while she closed the door, bumped the basket down the steps, and wheeled it down the—

Her limp was barely perceptible; the basket hid it.

"That's Rose Rossi," he said.

"Go ahead! We'll follow."

He poured money on the table for their tea and ran after her.

❧

Several blocks away was a blanchisserie, where laundry was collected before it was shipped off to the laundries at Courbevoie. She went in; he doubted for a moment; then she came back out, without the wheeled basket, hurrying, like a woman late for an appointment.

It was full dark and she was wearing a hat that shielded her face.

The street opened out on a little market square, an area of cobblestoned pavement; behind it was a church and an open space, half churchyard, half garden, separated from the street by a brick wall covered with ivy. By the church, a streetlight made rainbows in the wet air.

She was carrying a bundle. Her black coat, he guessed, and the veil.

There was a light in the churchyard too, a gaslight by the church itself.

Rose Rossi went into the churchyard.

He stood by the gate and watched her. The churchyard was almost English, with a few table tombs and a couple of huge old trees. On the bench, under the light, sat a woman in a nanny's white cap and black coat, knitting.

The nanny was an African woman. As she looked up, he saw a line of *dear G-d, are those cigarette burns* across her face.

A woman from the Congo. From the village that had lied for Rose.

And out of the churchyard darkness, bright on the gray stones, a top came spinning.

In the Paradis des enfants, Reisden had seen Rose Rossi buying thirty-six tops like it. In front of the church was an area of paving; the top spun, humming, then bounced and clattered as it found a crack in the stones. It jittered down the crack and bounced all the way toward the gate, past Rose Rossi who was just putting down her bundle.

And Reisden saw everything. He knelt and picked up the top and held it out to the little shape hesitating in the darkness.

"Hello, Philippe," he said. "Hello."

The child came forward into the light. A small claw reached out to take the toy. Reisden had just been having tea with Lucie Ray. He didn't flinch. He didn't look away.

"Show me how you spin it."

A small, horribly scarred face, but two good eyes, an inquisitive grin—and then Rose Rossi rushed at Reisden, screaming.

"You can't have him! You can't take him!"

She beat at his face. The nursemaid whipped her knitting off the needles and flourished the needles like a knife. "Run!" Rose Rossi screamed at her son. "Run, Philippe, get away!" Her wide-brimmed hat fell back, fell off, as she turned to fight him, to protect her son.

And her face was not burned at all.

"Why did she do it, darling?" Dotty asked.

All of them ended up back at Jouvet and talked until four in the morning. Little Philippe stared fascinated at Lucie Ray (*someone who looks like me!*) and at the human skull in the bookshelf and the gilded sphinxes, and petted the sphinxes' heads, and then fell asleep pillowed on his mother's coat and veil. The nursemaid took him off to nap.

"Why did you do it?" Reisden asked Rose.

"So Godefroy's mother wouldn't get him! I couldn't bear his being with Mathilde!" Rose Rossi sobbed.

And that was part of the French law of succession too. Not only the dowry, but the heir would have been part of the St.-Martin family. Under Mathilde de St.-Martin, who had raised Godefroy to be what he was.

"And I thought, if everyone thinks I'm burned, no one will marry me and I can take care of him forever. I never thought what people might *say*, I never thought—"

"Dear," Lucie Ray said, "you can't. You must face things and he must go to school soon."

"School!" his mother shuddered, and lowered her voice. "No. Never. They'll talk about *him*."

"Some will, dear, but you can't do bullies' work for them."

"There's a great deal that should be done for him," said Mme Herschner briskly, "grafts and exercises, a great deal. We can—" She broke off and looked at Reisden.

"I *can't*—" Rose Rossi covered her face with her red, seamed hands, bravely burned from having rescued her son, and whispered through them. "Go back into the world as if nothing had happened?" she said. "Take another husband, perhaps, who might be as bad as Godefroy?"

Had she killed Godefroy? They still didn't know. But she'd spent the past years accused of killing Philippe, and she'd been alone with it.

This he could do, and not as a murderer, just as a human being.

"You may count on his being teased at school," he said. "Everyone is. Count on his finding friends too. He'll think life isn't fair. It isn't. Your job is to tell him it isn't his fault what people think of him but it is his fault if he doesn't do his homework. You've been brave. Your job is to keep being brave for him. And ours—" *ours?* "our job," he continued grimly, "is to help you, and to make it quite clear to Godefroy's mother that Philippe will stay with you and *not* with her."

Rose Rossi bent over her hands, sobbing. "I can't do it," she whispered.

"You can't do it alone," said Lucie Ray.

"And what did the grandfather think?" Dotty asked.

"I took him a photograph."

Charles Rossi had flinched and stared somberly at it. It had taken him five minutes to say anything, but what he said in the end was "He's got his mother's eyes, doesn't he?"

Then he'd marched down the corridor and knocked at his daughter's door. It had been a minute, two minutes, three, before the door had opened. Rose had stood in the doorway, with Philippe clinging to her skirt.

"Daughter," Rossi had said. "Daughter."

Then he'd dropped to one knee and held out his arms. "I'm your grandfather, Philippe. Good to meet you. Did you know there are banana trees in this house? Would you like to see them?"

"And Godefroy's mother," Dotty said, "will she still make Rose Rossi testify?"

"No." Among Jouvet's experts, it turned out, were both a criminal lawyer and a specialist in cases like Godefroy's. "We all called on her with Mlle Nkulu," the nursemaid, "who had stories of her own." He remembered Mathilde de St.-Martin's avid hands flexing on her knees, her thick claw-pointed fingernails. "Mathilde's lawyer is advising her not to lay claim to the dowry."

"But now," Dotty said, "is Jouvet done with, and shall I have my building?"

"No," he said.

"Two months," he told Mme Herschner. "To see if you can make Jouvet work without Dr. Jouvet." He handed her a page of his own figures. They almost matched hers. "This is how much we'll need to make by then."

"Well, let's get started!" she said, and almost ran to her desk to begin telephoning.

"But darling," Dotty said. "Jouvet—"

"Yes, mad people," he said. "If I'm going to be a madman forever, *chère,* someone should get something out of it."

"But you *don't* have to—"

"Yes, I think I do. Dotty?" he said. "It's time to talk about Esmé."

She turned pale.

"You don't trust me with your troubles and I've given you reasons not to. But, darling? It's still me. I'm here. I will be here for you and Tiggy. Now will you kindly tell me what has happened between you and your foul husband?"

Dotty burst into tears. She couldn't speak. He simply held her, feeling her thin shoulders shake with sobs. "It's all right, Dots," he said. "We'll get through this together. We're family. It's all right."

∿

"But what about the toys and the orphans?" asked Paul Polin. "Where did they fit in?"

"Apart from her genuinely wanting to support them? Now there I was a master of deduction," Reisden said wryly. "I thought about those numbers for weeks and didn't see a thing. 21, 16, 36, 15. Unlikely numbers. One gives round numbers to a charity, doesn't one? 100 francs, not 97 or 102. I telephoned the orphanage. She gave the children toys in multiples of five and bought them in multiples of five plus one, and no one noticed. A way of giving him toys without anyone seeing. But no extra doll, because boys don't play with dolls, or so my nephew says. I should have seen it."

"You should?"

"She couldn't let anyone suspect Philippe was alive. She didn't care about the dowry. She only wanted to keep

Philippe away from Mathilde. Mlle Nkulu and her mother's esthetician were in on the secret. Mlle Nkulu nursed Philippe and smuggled him aboard the ship that brought Rose to France. He lived with Mlle Nkulu and Rose met him when she could."

"All that to keep him safe," Polin said. "Can you imagine?"

He could. The stratagems, the lies, the guilt, the exile alone behind the veil—She was young, still pretty, and she was innocent, and she'd given it all away for her son.

He had got his microscope back from Allard's that morning. He set it carefully on the bench and began constructing the dark-field lighting around it while Polin watched. He brought out his test slides to calibrate it, and sighed in relief and satisfaction.

"May I?" Polin brought out his own test slides. He clipped one of the slides in place and looked through the eyepiece, focusing it.

"Brilliant. Just brilliant," Polin said.

"About as good as one gets," Reisden said, and made a face. "With visible light."

The two of them looked at each other.

"With visible light," Polin agreed sadly.

"We'll have to think about that Zeiss UV, won't we?" Reisden said. "Lunch?"

❧

Jouvet would officially open for business again the week before Christmas. On the Sunday before, Reisden stripped down to shirtsleeves and old trousers and cleaned up Dr. Jouvet's apartment—which meant, literally, bringing a wheelbarrow up in the elevator, throwing things into boxes, and wheeling them down the hall to pile them in one of the spare bedrooms.

He had got to the unopened packages of books in the music room when Mme Herschner came up, bringing a carafe of coffee and two cups.

"When he was younger he would have read all those books," she said with a sad pride. "He read everything, went to the theatre or the opera every night. He was a musician. Such singing and playing there was up here! He even grew orchids."

"How did he get the piano in?" By which he meant, was it possible to get the piano out? He could still, constantly, imagine Perdita there.

"We had to take out a window and part of the wall."

"Then I suppose it stays."

Mme Herschner turned around and must have seen his face. "Monsieur le docteur?" she said. "Does the piano bother you?"

She held out a cup of coffee and he took it, cradling it between his hands for warmth. He'd told her he'd murdered someone. He could tell her this.

"There was a girl," he said. "In America last summer. I decided I loved her and I proposed marriage to her. I had no business doing it. Perdita's ten years younger than I am and considerably less...dented? And she's a pianist; the real thing, I think. She'd been accepted to a conservatory in New York. We went there to tell them she wouldn't be coming, but—" He shrugged. "She needed to be at the conservatory the way I need to be at Physio.Psych., and so she's there and I am here. I miss her."

"That doesn't last forever, the conservatory."

He shook his head. "She'll meet a nice young man who plays the violin. They'll acquire a cellist and form a piano trio. It wasn't love between her and me, I think. It was," he searched for a word, "gratitude, affection...whatever it was."

Mme Herschner nodded.

"I have family here. I have my work. I know who I am and what I should be doing. That's enough."

Mme Herschner just listened.

"Then why," he said, "why do I feel that, if I'd been infinitely more courageous, I wouldn't have decided I'd never need to see her or Gilbert again? Why do I wish every d—n time I see that piano that Perdita was sitting there?"

"That's perfectly normal," Mme Herschner said. "To get your mind back and not know what to do with it."

"It's *normal?*"

They looked at each other.

"Then why does it hurt?" he asked.

"Because you feel it."

∾

The morning Jouvet opened for business, the company gave an open house and everyone in Paris showed up. Charles Rossi had insisted on "sending over a few things to snack on"; every inch of Jouvet except the actual labs was bright with fruit bowls, *petits plats*, sandwiches, an enormous steam coffee machine served by two acolytes, and even a chef making crepes. Georges Allard was there, Polin, most of the people from Physio.Psych., little Fourche, who was dazed with pleasure at not needing to find a home for the archives.

And, strolling in as casually as if he weren't an arrondissement away from his home and lab, here came the boss of Physio.Psych. himself, Berthet.

"What a fine diversion!" he said, smiling.

"It's terrifying."

"It'll be a huge success!" Berthet said. "I'll see you at the lab."

"You will indeed."

The place was crowded with smiling people he didn't know. *Congratulations, Monsieur de Reisden! So glad, Monsieur le docteur!* He smiled and said the right things until he couldn't take any more and then he retreated upstairs to Dr. Jouvet's apartment.

What have I done, dear Heaven, what have I done?

Made a success, apparently. It was already likely that Jouvet would turn a profit on lab work alone. He would end up looking clever, the man from Physio.Psych. who'd picked up Jouvet from the gutter and realized it was a going concern.

(And was that why Berthet had shown up this morning? To lend Physio.Psych.'s blessing to Jouvet? Berthet had been a student of Dr. Jouvet... *Did he want me to do this?*)

And what would Jouvet do to him?

The apartment was his now; he'd live here. Today Jouvet was full of people celebrating. Tomorrow the waiting rooms would be full of the mad and desperate. He'd live above a madhouse.

Dotty hated the idea, and was probably right.

The sun was out, struggling through the dusty curtains and making a bright blade of sunshine on the rug. He pulled the curtains open, and after a moment went across to the velvet curtains covering the door to the music room and pulled those open too, and touched the piano.

Perdita, I miss you. He'd thought about her ever since he'd talked about her with Mme Herschner, as if he hadn't thought about her before. *I miss you and I will not get in your way. Have your life, have your violinist, have a splendid and wonderful life. Mine is all right. Good, really. I'm where I should be, doing what I should.*

But I miss you.

I will miss you all my life.

This wasn't the day to face that. He should go back downstairs. He put it off for a moment longer, going through the early morning mail. There was a note from Dotty.

Darling, I should <u>warn</u> you! Tiggy <u>insists</u> on giving you a present for Christmas, and you shouldn't <u>make fun of it</u>—

He would never make fun of anything Tiggy did.

He <u>insists</u> on giving you a <u>little stuffed bear</u>—

He looked at Dotty's note, astonished, smiling, remembering Tiggy picking out the jolly little bear with the red bow at the Paradis des enfants. *It's <u>very</u> important,* Tiggy had said. *It's <u>for</u> someone.*

Was *he* someone? To Tiggy?

He reached for a post card and scribbled on it: *That bear will delight me beyond measure.*

Five minutes more, and he'd need to go back downstairs. He looked across at the piano again. Perdita, I'd give you a stuffed bear. I'd give you a piano. I'd give you my heart.

There was one thing he could give her.

On the desk were pen and paper and a pile of unused stationery. *Dr. Jules Jouvet, chez Jouvet, rue de l'Université—*

He lined out Dr. Jouvet's name and wrote *Alexander Reisden.*

Dear Perdita—

It wasn't the sort of letter that one sends. One writes half of it, then puts it unfinished in a drawer and locks the drawer. When it came to reaching toward anyone, he was the world's coward; he wouldn't send it. But for five minutes he just talked on paper to her, a sort of Christmas letter. He told her about the lab, Berthet, Polin. *I've done something that surprised me—* He talked about buying Jouvet. He told her the story of Rose Rossi protecting her child Philippe, and how Jouvet would help them. *Jouvet was worth saving,* he wrote, and saw how a story that had been painful to experience could somehow find a happy ending.

There was a knock at the door: Mme Herschner. "I *am* coming down," he said guiltily.

She nodded and smiled. "Here's the midmorning mail. Which you can look at later, monsieur."

"Which I shall look at later," he agreed, and then saw, among the notes of congratulations, a packet from New York.

He knew her handwriting.

She'd written. She'd always been better at that sort of thing than he was.

He tore the packet open.

She'd sent a picture.

She was in an evening gown, sitting at an American piano, smiling. He had forgot how simply beautiful she was. He stood the picture up on the desk and looked back and forth from it to her letter.

Dear Alexander,

Here I am being a pianist! I am giving a very little concert and had to have my picture taken for the program, so I thought I would send you one. I'm wearing another girl's concert dress because mine wasn't ready, so imagine me with thirty-seven pins up and down my back.

Thank you, Alexander. You were right. I should be here.

But I miss our conversations. May I write you again and tell you what I'm doing? I understand why you might not want—

"Five minutes more," he said to Mme Herschner, sat down at the desk again, and took a fresh sheet of paper.

My dear Perdita— No. Not his. *My dear, my dear, my dearest Perdita,* no, you'll never hear that from me. But tell me your triumphs, tell me your happy endings; and I will do my best, my dear, to tell you mine.

Dear Perdita,

Tell me. Tell me everything.

ACKNOWLEDGMENTS

At the beginning of the pandemic, a group of women, mostly writers, got together on Zoom to share our stories, triumphs, frustrations, and recipes. We're still meeting. Thanks to Claire Murray, Robin Hansen, Zara Haimo, Robin Ray, and sometimes Kathryn Cramer and Marsha Finley. Without you, friends, life would be smaller, less interesting, and much less funny.

Thanks to the SinC writing groups, Claire Murray's Sunday and Monday salons, the London Writers' Salon, and all of us who've learned to write together and encourage each other. Hey, Zoom, we don't know what we'd do without you. We're such fans.

This novella has a long, circuitous history. It was originally written as a short story (!) and kept getting longer, and longer...as they do. Thanks to Stephen Rogers, Paula Messina, and the Cambridge Speculative Fiction Workshop—Steven Popkes, Alex Jablokov, Ken Schneyer, Gillian Daniels, Brett Cox, and James Cambias—for patiently reading it as it found a shape. Thanks to Verena Rose at Level Best Books and to the Black Orchid Novella contest for encouragement. (Wonder why Mme Herschner has an orchid and a rose on her desk? Wonder no longer.)

Thanks above all to my dear family my husband Fred Perry, kids Mariah and Justus, and their families. Much love to my brother Ken, who died just before this book was published; your memory is a blessing and makes me smile every time I think of you. XOXO to my sister Kathy and SIL Kathy, Kathy Texas and Kathy New Hampshire, and to their families, especially Matt Renner, Kaley Dvorak, and Dana Smith. We've shared a lot recently. Love you all.

And a special acknowledgment to Bear, who posed for the cover.

9 781951 636203